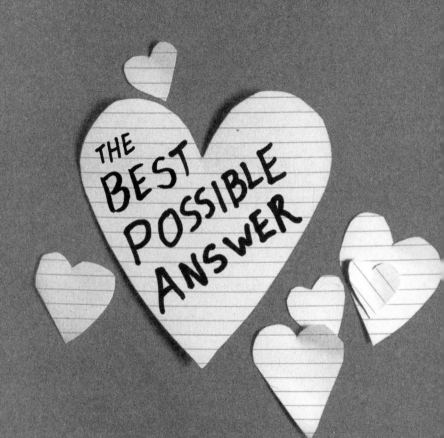

ALSO BY
E. KATHERINE
KOTTARAS

HOW TO BE BRAVE

THE
BEST
POSSIBLE
ANSWER

E. KATHERINE
KOTTARAS

ST. MARTIN'S GRIFFIN
NEW YORK

This is a work of fiction. All of the characters, organizations, and events portrayed in this novel are either products of the author's imagination or are used fictitiously.

Designed by Anna Gorovoy

www.stmartins.com

The Library of Congress Cataloging-in-Publication Data is available upon request.

ISBN 978-1-250-07281-8 (hardcover)
ISBN 978-1-4668-8468-7 (e-book)

Our books may be purchased in bulk for promotional, educational, or business use. Please contact your local bookseller or the Macmillan Corporate and Premium Sales Department at 1-800-221-7945, extension 5442, or by e-mail at MacmillanSpecialMarkets@macmillan.com.

First Edition: November 2016

10 9 8 7 6 5 4 3 2 1

To Matthew and Madeline

*Live the questions now. Perhaps then,
someday far in the future, you will gradually, without
even noticing it, live your way into the answer.*

—Rainer Maria Rilke

PART ONE

Viviana Rabinovich-Lowe's College Application Checklist

☐ May: AP Exams

☐ June–July: Design and Engineering Summer Academy

☐ August: Work on College Apps; Study for SAT

☐ September: Finalize Stanford Application

☐ October: SAT General Test;
   Submit Early Action Application to Stanford

AP Physics Exam: Sample Question

A girl is traveling home from the AP physics exam on her bicycle. She is traveling at x m/s and can stop at a distance d m with a maximum negative acceleration. If the bicycle travels at 2x m/s, which of the following statements are true?

(A) The girl is so stressed, exhausted, and overworked that she falls asleep while riding her bike.
(B) That's right; she loses momentum after taking a three-hour exam on the laws of gravity.
(C) The girl won't know for a few months how she did on the actual test.
(D) But it couldn't have been good, considering she couldn't get from point A to point B without falling on her face.
(E) All of the above.

You know the answer.

(Hint: Test-prep research shows you should actually always pick E.)

And now my mom wants me to *explain* that answer, not just mark the bubble black and call it a day. I also have to analyze data and make relevant observations and explain the process by which I've managed to land myself in a hospital room with a CT scan, a mild concussion, and a hideous gash on my forehead that probably makes me look like something out of *The Walking Dead*.

She stands at the edge of my bed, her face heavy with worry, her voice pained with the shame of what I've done, of who I am.

"How did you get to this place, Viviana?"

"How could you have done this, Viviana?"

"I can't take much more, Viviana."

I close my eyes and turn on my side. "I'm too tired to talk about it, Mama."

My little sister runs into the room and turns up the TV.

"Come on, Mila," my mom grunts at her. "Let's go." But before they leave the room, my mom leans over the bed and whispers in my ear: "We'll talk about this when we get home."

But I don't want to leave this bed. This bed has crisp white sheets and a soft fleece blanket. It smells like bleach, which smells like peace to me, and in it I can lie still and watch *Jeopardy!* on mute so I can guess without knowing what the contestants are saying or how condescending Alex Trebek is. It doesn't matter if I get the answers right or wrong—it only matters that I tried. There's a call button if I get thirsty or want Jell-O or an extra pillow, and I don't know my roommate's name, nor do I care, so long as she keeps her TV on mute, too.

In this room, there are fluorescent lights and beeping machines, but there is no phone with the interminable notifications and reminders, no AP or SAT study guides, no agenda, no laptops, no books. All that was confiscated from me the minute they checked me in. I wish they'd keep it all forever.

The doctor meets my mom right at the door so that they can consult about my "mental state of being." My mom closes the door halfway, and though she thinks she's whispering, I can hear every word. Maybe part of it is the cold familiarity of a hospital room, the fact that we've spent too much time in consultations about her own prognosis and ultimate fate, which has turned out good so far but is still yet unknown—her accent isn't usually that noticeable, but I can hear it's thicker with the stress of what I've done and where I am.

She's so very mad at me.

My chest starts to tighten with that light stabbing of anxiety that I've been feeling for months. It's a remnant of the Episode that brought me here.

I take three deep breaths.

That's what the nurses told me to do if I feel it coming on again.

But my lungs are cold and tight.

I have to force myself to settle down. Because I will not fall into panic. I will not lose control again.

Simply put, I don't have time.

I still have the AP English exam next week and finals and then getting packed for the Academy, not to mention fall SATs and summer reading lists and all my college applications.

I will not fail.

Not again.

"Psst. Vivi, you okay?" It's Mila, at the foot of my bed. She's snuck away from our mom. I don't open my eyes. I don't feel like talking to anyone.

She pokes my leg. "I know you're awake. You were just playing *Jeopardy!* You were wrong about the tiger question. The Sumatran is the smallest subspecies of tiger, not the Burmese." She's way too smart for an eight-year-old.

"I *literally* learned that from *National Geographic*," she continues in this fake grown-up voice she's recently taken on. "You want to watch when we get home tonight?"

My eyes are closed, but I can tell she's doing that thing where she stares at me to make me respond. I bet her tongue is out and her face is contorted. I try not to move. I try not to blink.

"Vivi, come on." She pokes me again. "Are you okay? Talk to me."

She may be smart enough to memorize long lists of animal facts, but she's too young to understand the long list of possible reasons for why I'm here today, why I'm stuck in panic mode, why I don't ever want to leave.

**AP English Language and Composition Exam:
Sample Free Response Question**

**Viviana Rabinovich-Lowe nearly cracked her
skull because she fell asleep while riding her
bicycle home from a Very Important Test that will
determine her Future Life Self.**

 **In a well-written essay, develop your position
with clear, detailed evidence to argue who is to
blame for this particular mess of a situation.**

*From the very early years, Viviana Rabinovich-Lowe's
father told her to work hard, to give nothing less than her
"very best." Even when she earned—EARNED, I say—
straight A's, he still insisted that she could "do better." He's
an engineer and should know. He made her promise not
to date until she was at least eighteen, until after she was
accepted into college (fingers crossed for Stanford, his alma
mater).*

Then, after she makes one mistake—one wrong choice, one missed bubble on the Scantron—he disappears— threatens to destroy his marriage, her family, the equilibrium of everything she knows. He didn't care that her mother—his wife of twenty years, the so-called love of his life—looked death in the eye—thyroid cancer—and won. Instead, he moved halfway around the world to build skyscrapers in Singapore without explaining why. He didn't care about leaving a recently very sick woman. He didn't care that his daughters needed him, that Viviana needed him.

Of course, then, her father must be to blame.

However, upon second thought, perhaps Viviana Rabinovich-Lowe's mother is no better. She won't admit it, but she's just as disappointed and embarrassed. She's always sided with Viviana's father when he pushed her. Her mother, for her part, likes to remind Viviana of how much she's survived. How her family left the former Soviet Union when she was thirteen. How she spent her prime teen years in flux, without a real home. How the government promised them a new, better life, but they became stuck in the middle of an international tug-of-war, simply because they were Jewish. How they waited eleven months stuck in middle-of-nowhere Italy, not knowing what was to become of them, before the governments finally allowed her family to leave. She came to the U.S. so Viviana could have a better life than her. All Viviana's heard, her entire sixteen years, is that she has to work hard, be grateful, do her absolute best, make her proud.

It's too much pressure, these stories.

It's too much to take in.

Therefore, her mother must be to blame.

However, then there's Viviana Rabinovich-Lowe's ex-boyfriend, Dean Andrews. Apparently, Viviana's BFF Sammie always knew he was the biggest ass on the North Side of Chicago (perhaps even all of Illinois, perhaps even all of North America, Canada and all). During their late-night Binocular and Braiding Sessions, Sammie repeatedly reminded Viviana of that fact. She said so from the very start, that he's totally and completely to blame.

While the evidence presented above is thorough and complicated and nuanced with the conflicting emotions of all those involved, do not be swayed by such arguments. They are only part of the mess, not the main contributor to it.

The bottom line is: Viviana Rabinovich-Lowe is, ultimately, the most at fault. Her father warned her; her mother begged her; her own best friend questioned her life choices.

But did she listen? Of course not.

Instead, she took on a boyfriend—she's the one who made the choice to succumb to that distraction, and then to send him that picture (no one forced her). She had other, more important things she should have been focusing on.

Instead of accomplishing the very best, she's sunk to her absolute worst.

"Viviana, talk to me." Mila's voice sounds small again, scared. "What happened? Mom won't tell me. Are you going to be okay?"

I roll over and open my eyes. "Hi."

"Hi." Her little face is full of worry. She's a tiny version of my mom, with her big dark eyes and stick-straight bob. I look nothing like either of them. I inherited my dad's light eyes and wild red hair. But Mila and I both inherited my mom's ability to worry. I suppose it's better than inheriting his ability to flee. "Are you sick?"

"Kind of. Not really. I just fell and bumped my head." I don't mention the blacking out or the concussion or the choking feeling that won't go away. "I'll be okay."

"I can take care of you tonight," she says. "You can lie on the couch, and we can watch whatever you want. I'll be your nurse, get you juice, and take your temperature and stuff." She strokes my hair, as if doing that could erase everything that's happened. "I'll get you anything you want, anything at all."

All I want is to be left alone. I probably, really, most likely, absolutely did fail that exam today, but if there's one thing I did learn from my physics class, it's that an object at rest wants to remain at rest. I want to remain at rest.

I want to resist motion.

I want inertia.

But I know that's not an option right now.

There is no option F.

"Thanks, Mila," I say. "Right now, I just want to sleep a little."

"Okay," she says, but then she sits down next to me and continues to pet my head. I wish she'd leave the room, let me be.

I don't say anything.

Instead, I close my eyes and try not to cry.

Habits of an Effective Test Taker #1

Find a study buddy, someone you can trust, someone who can really push you to do your best work. Have that person test you on the material so that you uncover your weaknesses. Make sure you return the favor!

We get home, and I immediately text Sammie to come down. She lives above us on the seventeenth floor, and I'm feeling especially grateful that the only fully normal human being I know lives a mere forty seconds away via an emergency stairwell.

She lets herself into our apartment with her key. We lock my bedroom door so my mom can't nosy her way in. "What happened to you? I've been texting you all day."

We climb into my bed and lean our backs against the

window that overlooks all of Chicago. I fill her in on my accident, how my mom had to leave her Constitutional Law class and how obviously annoyed she was about all of it. How my dad, away on what has become a six-month business trip, hasn't even returned my mom's calls to see if I'm okay. "Once again, I've proved that I can't do anything right."

"I'm sorry." Sammie reaches over to me and gives me a hug.

"The doctors say I need therapy."

Sammie shrugs. "I went to group counseling after my dad died. It helped to talk to someone. It's just talking."

That's easy for her to say, but my mom is skeptical of things like therapy and counseling. When the ER doctor handed her a printed list of local psychologists along with my discharge papers, my mom visibly winced. "It's like one hundred and fifty bucks a session," I say. "So, I don't know. I mean, we probably can't afford it anyway."

"Well, you can always talk to me."

"At least I'll be out of here in a few weeks." When I was in the eighth grade, I announced that I wanted to be an engineer, like my dad, so he immediately signed me up for the Illinois State Design and Engineering Summer Academy. I spent the last two summers in a downtown day camp program learning about things like computer modeling, design thinking, data acquisition, and structural analysis. This summer, since I'm going into my senior year, I'm going to be staying on campus two hours away as part of the residential program.

Sammie pouts. "I'm going to miss you."

I lean my head on her shoulder. "I'm going to miss you

more," I say, though the truth is, I'm looking forward to getting away from home.

My mom knocks on the door. I slink down onto my pillow, and Sammie unlocks the door to let her in. My mom approaches the bed and places her hand on my forehead, as if I were a child with a slight fever and something as simple as a small dose of Tylenol would make me feel better, as if she could make all the discomfort go away. "You need to go to sleep."

"Mama, I've been sleeping all day."

My mom frowns. "The doctors said you work too hard, that you've made yourself sick."

"Please, I don't want to talk about it."

"But, Viviana, I don't like how you—"

"Mama, I'm fine." I tell her that I don't need anything, that I have Sammie to watch over me, that I will go to sleep if she'd just leave me be. Sammie nods, and finally my mom leaves.

Sammie crawls into bed next to me. "She's pretty upset."

"Let's not talk about it anymore?"

"Whatever you want."

I roll over and look out the window at the city outside. "Tell me a story?"

"Sure," Sammie says, and reaches for the binoculars, but then she stalls before she picks them up. "You want me to braid your hair?"

"No thanks," I say, and point to my bandage. "Headache."

"Right," she says, and then she picks up my binoculars to peer into other people's apartments.

I lean my forehead against the cold glass. Bennett Tower

is shaped so that a whole section of it juts out, which means that we can peek into the windows of people we don't know. We've been doing our Binocular and Braiding Sessions since we were kids, spying on our neighbors, making up stories about them, all the while braiding each other's hair. Of course, it started as a way for us to see if we could see anyone naked (we were ten)—and for sure, we've seen plenty. In fact, we've seen many things over the years: drunken brawls, late-night parties, and, yes, even sex. (It was under the covers, so I didn't really learn anything beyond what I could see on TV, and it was way more tame than anything on the Internet.) But now it's evolved into a bit of a pastime, with Sammie giving them all names and filling in intricate details about their lives. It's just the right distraction.

Sammie lifts her binoculars two stories above us. "The O'Briens are eating pizza again."

"Again?" The O'Briens have four little kids who do nothing but play video games and eat frozen food. "They're so boring."

She scans down a few floors. "The Nut's painting another self-portrait."

"The Nut" is what Mila calls this strange guy who lives a few floors below us in Bennett Tower with his nervous Chihuahua, whose amber eyes and pointy pink ears shake, even if it's ninety-five degrees outside. He spends most nights out on his balcony, painting, usually pictures of himself.

We always see him in the elevator, and he's usually talking to himself. Mila named him the Nut after we got stuck in the elevator with him last year. He spent all eleven floors cracking pistachios, throwing the shells on the floor, twitching and mumbling. It's hard to get an eight-year-old not to stare at adults who are testing the boundaries of appropriate behaviors themselves.

After we left the elevator and he was safely out of distance, Mila started singing this song she had learned at Girl Scouts. "Called myself on the telephone, just to see if I was home. Made a date for half past eight. Better hurry, or I'll be late. I'm a nut, I'm a nut, I'm a nut, nut, nut."

I tried to explain to her that he probably struggles with mental issues, but she wouldn't listen. She sang that annoying song for two days straight, until our dad finally made her stop, saying she had a lovely singing voice but that she really needed to vary her repertoire.

Sammie moves the binoculars left. "Ooh. Mrs. Woodley is doing Pilates on her balcony."

Mrs. Woodley's real name isn't Mrs. Woodley. Sammie made up her name, just as she did the O'Briens' and those of all the other people whose lives we spy on. We don't know Mrs. Woodley's real name, but she's a fifty-something-year-old woman who lives alone in an apartment on the tenth floor. For years, Mrs. Woodley was also a pretty boring character—she mostly just watched TV and ate microwave dinners. But recently she seems to be undergoing a renaissance of sorts—we've caught her belly dancing, cooking full gourmet meals and then eating them alone, and now, doing Pilates on the balcony.

I peek out the window. "She's wearing her new purple leotard."

"And she changed her hair. She looks good as a brunette," Sammie says. "Hey. She's seeing someone."

"How do you know?"

Sammie hands me the binoculars. "Look at the dining room table."

I adjust the focus. "Oh my God. A dozen roses? Who do you think sent them?"

Sammie takes the binoculars from me. "A younger man. Most definitely. His name is Tad. Her personal trainer. He's in his early thirties, is muscular as all hell, and is taken by the fact that he's made her come alive."

"You're a hopeless romantic."

Sammie smiles at me. "Forever and ever," she says, and then she yells, "Go Mrs. Woodley!" She sort of screams this through the window, as though Mrs. Woodley could hear it. "She's had a hard, lonely life. I'm glad she's finally happy."

Sammie's stories are all fairy tales that lead to happy endings. I know she's trying to make me feel better, but for some reason, this story makes me feel a little worse.

Around ten, Sammie texts her mom that she's going to stay down here tonight. I place the binoculars on the sill, and she shuts off the lights. She crawls under the blanket next to me and plays with her phone a little before she falls asleep.

I lie next to the window and stare out at the city, the flashing lights, the endless cars, the buildings. I think about the O'Briens, the Nut, Mrs. Woodley, each of them busy and empty and desperately wanting more.

I wonder what they think when they look through our window.

I wonder if they've seen the fights, the tears, the sudden disappearance of my father.

I wonder what story it is that they tell about us.

Habits of an Effective Test Taker #2

Do not spend too much time on any one problem. Your anxiety might start building and then you'll lose focus. It's better just to move on.

My mom makes the announcement over breakfast.

"I have made up my mind. You are not going." She says this as she spreads marmalade on her toast, all calm and quiet.

It doesn't fully process at first. Sammie's gone back up to her apartment to get ready for school, and Mila's still in her pajamas. The sun isn't up yet. I haven't poured sugar into my coffee. I haven't even taken a sip.

"Mama, what are you talking about?"

She puts down her knife and looks at me. "It's too expensive. We cannot afford it. And it is too much work for you. The doctors say you work too hard. You've made yourself sick."

"Are you talking about the Engineering Academy?" It's just too early to fully comprehend the context of what my mom is saying.

"Of course I am talking about the Engineering Academy. I have made my decision and you cannot argue with me. I'm not allowing you to go." She picks up her mug to take a sip of her coffee. She's still cool and calm and quiet.

But I'm instantly awake.

And my mind is anything but quiet.

The anxiety rushes over me harder than caffeine. The sweat, the heart palpitations, the tears. "Mama, no," I start to plead. "I'm going. I have to go."

"No." She slams her coffee mug down on the table, but her voice is still steady.

"But we need to talk to Dad. He won't agree with you. He wants me to go—"

"No. I will not pay for it, and neither will your father. I have already talked to him. We can get a refund, and it is done."

"What? You talked to Dad?" My dad's had to go on business trips since I was little, but this is the longest he's ever been away, and I don't know what's happening with him and my mom. "When?"

"I'm sorry, Viviana. I spoke to him last night."

"Mama, please—"

"You will stay home and rest this summer."

Mila gets excited. "I want to stay at home, too! I want to stay home with Vivi!" I know she would be perfectly happy to stay home from Camp Sportz, where she said the third and fourth graders were mean to her last summer, but that's not what we had planned.

"I can't just sit around all summer doing nothing. It won't look good on my college applications."

"You're not going back," my mom says. "End of discussion."

"*Please*, Vivi," Mila begs. "Let us both stay home. We'll have so much fun."

My mom shakes her head and says something to herself in Russian and then finally instructs Mila to get her bag together for school. After Mila's left the room, my mom turns back to me. "It's been too much, Viviana. Didn't you hear anything the doctors said? They told you to slow down. You need to slow down."

She can't do this to me. She can't just strip away the only good thing I have.

But she can.

I can't speak. I can't breathe.

I try to force out the words: "I don't need to slow down. I don't want to slow down. I can fix this—"

She throws her hands up. "You haven't been making good decisions. Not at all. So I will make the decision for you." And then she half-whispers at me: "We need to keep a close eye on you. You are not living away at a camp for that long. We need to know we can trust you. Right now, you're a bad role model for your little sister."

I know what this dig is about.

I know it's not about the fall or my academic stuff or even my health.

I know it's really about what I did with Dean.
She's caught me. And there's nothing I can say.
She's made her decision.
And so has my father, apparently.
Without even talking to me.

Habits of an Effective Test Taker #3

Effective test takers are honest with themselves about how much effort they're willing to put in to do well on the exam. It's true that you can learn anything, but you have to be willing to commit to doing the work.

My mom makes sure I've calmed down before she and Mila leave for school. She makes me promise not to study for the other AP exams I have next week. I lie and say that I won't.

After they leave, I text Sammie to tell her the news. She's already on the bus on her way to school, but she texts back that she's sorry and wishes she could do something for me.

And then, I'm alone. I try to study for the AP English exam that's next week, but I can't. I try to read, to memorize the definitions of all the tropes and schemes, but it's all a blur. So I stay true to my promise to my mom and I close the book. I head outside and sit on our balcony. We live on the sixteenth floor in a three-bedroom apartment that my parents rent. But that might be one of the other things we'll lose if my father doesn't come back and they decide to divorce. I might as well enjoy it before it's all gone.

I never do this. I never just sit. I lean my forehead against the iron railing and identify the patterns of the buses, cars, and people below me. The city below me wakes up. I start thinking about ant trails and power lines and circuitry connections, about the difference between a meandering labyrinth and a strategic maze. In the Design and Engineering Academy, we had to memorize the different patterns of nature, like the spirals and whorls that communicate regeneration and connectivity, and tessellating shapes that stack and pack and communicate stability and organization. We were instructed to use these patterns in our own designs, and the lessons are ingrained in me. My mind won't turn off. I can't just see the cab as a cab or the bus as a bus. Instead, I see how they move, how they're designed, how they could be improved.

My father would love this.

If he were here.

I wish that he were here.

I try to just watch the clouds, but even they make me think about energy and movement and space.

And physics exams.

And failure.

The Academy.

My mom talked to my dad. They talked about me. They talked about what they want for me.

I haven't talked to my dad in three months. He won't communicate with me to tell me why he left, why he's not coming home. I can't think of any other reason why he left so suddenly.

I don't know how to fix this.

And then come the palpitations. They flutter inside my chest.

It's happening again. The panic. The worry. The dizzying nausea. The caving in.

I go inside and crawl into my bed, try to breathe like they told me to at the hospital.

Deep breaths. Belly breaths, they said.

I try, but in my belly there's this pit of regret and disgust and exhaustion, and breathing into it only makes it worse.

I should call someone.

I shouldn't have been left alone.

I close my eyes.

I fall into the waves.

I melt into the bed.

I'm alone.

The Episode lasts for what feels like hours. When it finally calms down, I move to the couch and fall asleep to old episodes of *The Big Bang Theory* until it's time to pick up Mila.

She runs out of the gate toward me with a hand-drawn card made out of construction paper, and it's taped shut with daisy and unicorn stickers. "Here's your get-well card." And then she places her hand on my forehead. "You still look sick. Can we play nurse today?"

We get home, and I climb into bed so she can bring me a glass of milk and toast. She pulls out a doctor kit from when she was in preschool and listens to my heart with her plastic stethoscope.

I open the get-well card she drew for me. It's a picture of all of us—my mom, my dad, Mila, and me. We're stick figures standing in front of a two-story house, smiling and holding hands.

My heart drops. Ever since she was in kindergarten, when her teacher gave her an assignment to find out what her parents did for work, she's asked our dad the same question: "When will you build us a house?" He always laughs and tries to explain that he doesn't build houses, that he works on large skyscrapers in foreign countries, but it never appeases her. "But you could if you wanted to," she always says. "You know how."

This house is nothing like where we live. It has a slanted roof, a picket fence, and a chimney. There's a green yard with apple trees and purple flowers, and a rainbow arcs over our round and smiling heads. It's nothing like Bennett Tower, where we actually live, with its cold white stone and black balconies, an ugly old skyscraper that just straight up out of the earth.

Mila leans over my shoulder. "Sorry it's not perfect."

"Mila, why do you say it's not perfect?"

"I wanted to make it right for you. But I had trouble with the arms."

"Mila, come on. I love it. And you know there's no such thing as perfection."

She pauses for a moment. "I think you're perfect. I think Mommy's perfect." She doesn't mention our dad.

My Academy teachers said that we're asymmetrical beings seeking a perfect kind of symmetry that can never be attained. They showed us cracked vases as examples of the beauty of ordinary objects. No design is perfect, they said, but we still can't help but try.

I look at Mila's drawing. My arms have been drawn and erased so many times, I look like the ghost of a Hindu god. "How about this?" I say. "I think that your picture *is* perfect because you made it."

"I guess," she says.

I get out of bed so I can pin it to the bulletin board above my desk, but then she grabs it from me and rips it in two.

"What are you doing?"

"I'll make you a new one tomorrow," she says, crumpling the pieces as she runs.

"But I like that one!" I chase after her down the hallway and try to pull it from her grasp, but when I finally release it from her hands, it's completely destroyed.

The next day is Saturday, which means I basically get a four-day weekend, if you include the fabulous ER visit. But it also means that my mom's home and is on guard to make sure that I do nothing but rest. I have to watch *Wild Kratts* with Mila while my mom studies at the dining room table.

There she is, stressing about her classes, all the while watching over me like the hawk that Mila's obsessed with on her program.

At noon, I get a text from Sammie telling me to come upstairs, that she has news—"big, big news!"

My mom lets me go so long as I promise "no reading, no studying."

It takes me thirty-eight seconds to reach Sammie's apartment via the emergency stairwell. She's standing at the door, jumping and smiling and clapping her hands.

"What's up?"

"You're going to work with me this summer!" She yells this, and her mom tells her to close the door, that she's going to wake up the entire building.

"What are you talking about?"

"I got you a job."

The building we live in is part of this microcosm of a neighborhood called Bennett Village, which isn't really a village, not like the small town outside of Kiev where my mom grew up. Bennett Village is just a five-block stretch of land in the middle of Chicago where four identical highrises are separated by overpriced town houses and courtyards that have more concrete than plant life. It was built fifty years ago and was part of this idyllic postwar desire to achieve the American dream, according to my dad, who knows these things. Our building towers over a private Olympic-size outdoor pool on the ground floor, where Sammie worked last summer. Even if you live in the village, you still have to pay a hefty fee to the condo association in order to use the pool.

As it turns out, Mrs. Salazar is in with Mr. Bautista, the head of Bennett Village maintenance. Sammie's Filipina, and she has a huge family who live all over Chicago, including Mr. Bautista, who's her dad's second cousin through marriage. He trusts Sammie's mom, so he agreed to hire me without even a pretend interview.

"My mom's not going to approve," I say. "She wants me to sit and do nothing."

"You will be doing nothing, though. You'll be sitting around, with me, *getting paid* to just hang out!"

Sammie is absolutely elated. She has extremely high hopes for the summer. "I'm telling you," she says. "It will be awesome, the summer of our lives. Sun, water, hot guys, free days at the pool. What more could you want?"

"To go to the Illinois Design and Engineering Summer Academy."

"I get that. But that's not happening, obviously. And anyway, don't you want to spend the summer with me?"

I think about it. It is a tempting option. At least a job will look better on college applications than saying I stayed home all summer doing nothing. And it will still give me time to study for my SATs, which I need to retake in the fall. "Yes, of course I do," I say. "But my mom's not going to like it. She wants to keep a close eye on me."

"How is she going to keep an eye on you? She's going to be in class."

"She's going to force me to stay home."

"Let's go talk to her." Sammie convinces me to let her go back downstairs with me to tell my mom.

My mom's annoyed—first, that Sammie's involving

herself in my recovery, and, even worse, that it's thwarting her plan to force me to rest, which is to say her plan to force me to stay at home so she can keep a close eye on me. "I don't want her wearing herself out again."

"Mr. Bautista said we could share a lot of our shifts. We'll mostly just be sitting around together. It'll be great. And very relaxing for Vivi."

"So, total inertia?" I ask.

"I don't know what that means," she says. Sammie's good at many things—English, history, Drama Club, choir, and secret fashion blogging (1,428 IG followers, and if her mom knew, she'd kill her)—but one of her many things is not science. I'm not a science genius either, but I've absorbed enough to recite the basics.

"Like in physics," I say. "One definition of inertia is the tendency to remain at rest. To resist movement."

"Yes. Like that. I want Viviana to resist all movement. I want her to 'remain at rest.'" My mom echoes me. "And to stop thinking so much."

"We will absolutely resist all movement," Sammie says. "And we'll be right downstairs, only fifteen floors away. We will sit at the front desk and do nothing but check IDs and listen to music."

"That is all? No lifeguarding? No swimming, running, all of that?"

"No, Ms. Rabinovich. None of that."

"And you'll be right downstairs?"

"Yes. Right downstairs."

Mila whines from the couch. "No, please no! If Vivi goes to work, then that means I have to go to Camp Sportz."

I ignore Mila and offer my counterargument: "Instead of costing money," I say, "I'll actually be making money." I know she likes a good argument, and I hope it works.

"It will be summer job perfection, Ms. Rabinovich."

"I think this is a good compromise, Mama. I really want to do this."

My mom looks at me. "You think you're okay to do this?"

I think about what I thought was going to be my summer first—dorm life, late-night pizza, field trips, 3-D printers, fabrication labs, group presentations. Yes, it sounded fun, but I was doing it because it was something amazing to put on my college applications. This new possibility of a summer—blue skies, chlorine, whole days with Sammie— I have to admit that I actually feel some of the tension release from my shoulders. "Yes," I say. "I think this could be really good for me."

My mom sighs and then finally relents. "Okay, I guess. Fine. I'll have to talk to your father about this, but—"

"Thank you, Mama." I kiss her on the cheek and grab Sammie's hand so we can leave before she changes her mind. I hear Mila crying behind us, and I feel bad, but I don't turn back.

AP U.S. History Exam: Sample Question

Between October and December of last year, Viviana Rabinovich-Lowe engaged in romantic activities that directly opposed her parents' rules and expectations for how she was supposed to live her life. Analyze the reasons that these activities emerged in this period, and assess the degree to which Viviana succeeded in ruining both her social and her personal life.

Before Viviana started dating Dean early last October, her father warned her not to get involved with anyone. He said that "boys would be a distraction," that they'd take her off course from everything she'd worked for her entire life.

She didn't listen, of course.

She fell for Dean during a particularly bad day. Their physics teacher, Mr. Foster, had them in the computer lab, where they were working on an online roller-coaster simulator. Viviana had a C- in the class, so Mr. Foster thought that it would be a good idea to quiz her in front of everyone as a way to encourage her to raise her grade. He started riding her for not being able to explain the measurements of potential energy and kinetic energy as they related to her design. She thought she knew the answer, but everything that came out of her mouth was wrong. Rather than call on someone else, Mr. Foster kept picking on her. "Come on, Viviana. Think, Viviana. You know this, Viviana."

He wouldn't let up, and she wanted to cry so badly. Finally, rather than break down sobbing in front of the whole class, she put her head down and closed her eyes. Mr. Foster finally sighed and said, "Viviana, if you'd only apply yourself a bit more, you'd do well in this class."

She did everything she could not to let the other kids hear her cry. She choked it back, let the tears fall onto the desk.

Then she felt a tap on her shoulder and a note slide under her elbow.

It was from Dean, who had just transferred to their school from the suburbs a few weeks before. It was a quickly sketched cartoon with the two of them riding a roller coaster, and above his little figure, it said, "Let's convert our potential energy into kinetic together."

She lifted her head, wiped her tears, and smiled at him.

With that one little note and one kind smile, she was all in. She fell for him, and fast.

But her parents hated Dean from the very start. Her dad

called him "a useless distraction," while her mother reminded her constantly that she needed to focus on school.

Of course, she ignored them. She was able to hang out with Dean and even get her physics grade up to a B+. She was experiencing all kinds of firsts: first date, first kiss, first show-me-a-little-of-this, first hold-me-a-little-like-that. They tripped over the words "I love you" at first and then said them again and again. And then they explored and played and learned about each other's bodies. Dean wanted more, of course. He'd already had sex with his ex-girlfriend, and he said he was "hungry" for her. She wasn't ready yet, but she was completely okay with doing other stuff—playing and flirting and trying nearly everything but.

So last year, right after Thanksgiving, she took a picture of herself, a very private and personal picture that was supposed to be for his eyes only. She sent it to him via this new app called HushDuo, which was supposed to be this messaging system that was truly secure, unlike Snapchat. It was her idea. And he sent her one, too. She knew what she was doing. She liked what she was doing. He said he liked it, too. He said it was enough.

And she was in complete control.

Until she wasn't.

When Sammie texted her a photo of Dean making out with some girl at Alex Luna's New Year's Eve party, she broke up with Dean that night. She forwarded Dean the photo of his lying face sucking on that girl, along with one simple message: "We're done."

Even though she cried for four days, her parents seemed more relieved than anything that "this phase" was over.

But she was broken. She'd loved him. Or at least she thought she had. Certainly, she had trusted him with everything she was, everything she had.

Unfortunately, the lesson wasn't over quite yet.

Just her luck that Dean rigged his phone so he could save what was supposed to have been erased. Of course, Hush-Duo wasn't so secure after all. He didn't write back to her, but he did forward that very private and very personal photo to a few of his friends. Someone posted it on Instagram, someone else on Facebook, and after that, it spread like wildfire. By the time she returned to school in January, she couldn't walk down the hall without a whisper or a comment thrown her way. Because of Dean, she developed a reputation, and it was the antithesis of the hardworking, studious nerd that she'd been before. Suddenly, she was known as a "whore" and a "slut" and all kinds of other horrifying names the kids at school threw at her. Even her teachers gave her terrible looks. Instead of picking on her, Mr. Foster couldn't even look her in the eye.

But the worst part wasn't even that.

The worst part was when her parents got called into the principal's office. The worst part was when they saw the photo and read the comments. The worst part was sitting in that stiff leather chair waiting for her father's reaction. The worst part was his cold, empty stare, the fact that she'd failed him completely, that "this phase" had ruined her completely.

When he left five days later, she broke down. They came home from returning Christmas presents at Water Tower to find his desk empty, his closets mostly cleared out, no explanations, no good-byes. This wasn't just a weeklong business trip. This was different.

That was the absolute worst.

She learned that her parents were right. She learned that she'd ruined her life, completely. She learned that love is a distraction. She learned not to love, not to trust, and not to—ever again—let anyone else in.

PART TWO

Viviana Rabinovich-Lowe's College Application Checklist

☐ ~~May: AP Exams~~ *bombed*

☐ ~~June–July: Design and Engineering Summer Academy~~ *thwarted*
☐ July: *Work on College Apps*
☐ August: ~~Work on College Apps;~~ Study for SAT

☐ September: Finalize Stanford Application

       Take
☐ October: SAT General Test;
   Submit Early Action Application to Stanford

College Admissions Tip #1

Extracurricular and summer activities demonstrate your enthusiasm for the experience of learning. What's even more important is that you grow from the experience in new and important ways, and that you communicate that growth in your college essays.

The very first day of Bennett Tower Pool's Memorial Day Weekend Grand Opening is the exact opposite of inertia.

It's chaos.

Pure and utter chaos.

It's early Saturday morning, and the gate isn't even open yet, but the line outside is already packed with screaming kids, frantic mothers, oblivious fathers, and retired old couples desperate to get in. I've lived here for five years, but

I don't recognize anyone. Perhaps that's equally due to my life as a hermit.

Mr. Bautista leads us to our permanent post at the front desk, where we'll be scanning membership cards, checking IDs, recording visitors' passes, and selling snacks, and then he promptly checks his phone. "I've got a leaky faucet on the twenty-fifth floor. You'll introduce your friend to everyone, Sammie?"

"Will do," Sammie says, and he disappears.

I put my textbooks down on the counter. "I thought he was in charge?"

"He's in charge of the Bennett Village maintenance, but Virgo is the pool manager."

Virgo, who's placing towels on a shelf, hears his name and comes over. "Got yourself an accomplice this year, Sammie?"

"Yeah," she says. "Virgo, this is Viviana Rabinovich-Lowe."

"Viviana, you say?" He rolls the *r*'s and accents the *a*'s perfectly. "*Ciao, bella!* Are you, by chance, Italian?"

"No," I say. "My mom is Jewish, born in Russia, but she spent time in central Italy." I briefly explain the history of my mom's journey around the world. "They were only there for a few months when she was young, but she still gave my sister and me Italian names, she loved it there so much."

"Do you speak?"

I shake my head. My mom knows Russian, Hebrew, some Yiddish, and even a little Italian, and yet she never speaks any of the languages to us. My dad tried to convince her to speak to me ("Stanford loves multilingual students!"), but she refused. She never really does anything cultural or religious with us. Except for telling us her story, she says she wanted to leave those worlds behind.

"*Poverino!* Viviana!" Virgo, who has to be at least six feet tall, starts to sing my name in a gorgeous operatic voice. My name reverberates over the empty pool and into the sky. "The most beautiful operas in the world are Italian."

"Don't listen to him. He's Colombian but thinks he's from Rome."

"Actually, I'm from Irving Park, born and raised. But yes, my full name—Virgilio—is Italian, and so I am Italian in my soul," Virgo says, pressing his hand on his heart.

"He also thinks he's in charge," Sammie says. "But he's not the one signing your paycheck."

"I am very much in charge." Virgo puts his hands over my ears. "Ignore her. Listen to me. Listen to everything I say, *Signorina* Viviana. I know everything about everything."

"He doesn't know anything." A tall girl in a red sweatshirt and matching red shorts, with a sleek black ponytail that hangs all the way down her back, is sweeping the entrance.

"You can listen to her." Sammie gives her a hug. "Vanessa's pretty trustworthy."

I give a wave. "Nice to meet you, too."

Virgo calls a few of the other guards over to meet me: Vanessa's a junior, like Sammie and me, and Marquis is a senior who's just about to graduate. There are a few other guards who aren't here today, but I'll meet them tomorrow. I also find out that Virgo's home after his first year in college, and that he's studying music, of course.

Thankfully, everyone here is from a private school, and

it's a relief to be surrounded by people who don't know me, who don't know about what happened after the physics exam, and, best of all, who don't know about Dean and me.

It's a relief to be anonymous.

I wave hello, and they all smile. They all seem nice. And sun-kissed. And shiny.

While it's nice to be anonymous, I'm also suddenly self-conscious, aware of how pasty I am after spending the last three years holed up in a library or a lab.

"And who is this?" a new voice asks behind me.

I turn to the guy who's just made his way through the front gate, and oh no—

I know him.

Or at least I knew him once—as a younger, seventh-grade version of myself kissing a younger, ninth-grade version of him. Evan something or another—I can't remember his last name. But I do remember Seven Minutes in Heaven at Anne Boyd's birthday party. It was dark, and I was a little tipsy from the one and only beer I've ever dared to taste, and there were all these strange new boys from the private school up the road. I was overjoyed when Evan and I got paired together. I'd never kissed a boy before. And I thought there was no way he would want to kiss me. We sat in the dark on the edge of the tub, and finally, at six minutes forty-five seconds, I leaned in, and he leaned back. I tasted Bud Light and peppermint gum and his cold, chapped lips.

It was fifteen seconds of heaven. And then I never saw him again.

Until now.

I remember his short dark hair. Those ridiculous dimples and sharp brown eyes. And now he's tall, with broad shoulders. Naturally lean but also muscular. And yeah, his shirt is off, so there's that. Four years have been good to him.

"I'm Evan." He puts out his hand to take mine.

He doesn't remember me.

There are four forces in nature that act upon us. Gravity, of course, binds us to the earth. Electromagnetism binds our atoms together. The strong force binds the nucleus, and the weak force governs subatomic decay. Unless you've spent the past eight months obsessing over the AP physics exam and the past two years thinking about the design of physical structures and the risk of collapse, you don't normally think about these forces. You can't see them, and you certainly can't control them. They just happen. All you can do is observe.

When Evan puts his hand in mine, I'm inclined to believe there's a fifth force. It can't be defined or calculated or memorized, but it pulls me toward him. It's pulled me toward him before.

And there's something about him—the sincerity of his smile, the way he looks at me, direct and piercing, the strength of his hand around mine. I search his face to see if he remembers, too.

But when Sammie introduces me, he continues to give me a blank, open smile. "That's right—the BFF we never got to meet. You live here in Bennett, right? Why have we never been graced with your presence before?"

"I wanted to come down," I say. "I mean, Sammie invited me. I was just too busy—"

"Vivi's been too busy geeking it up at a physics academy," Sammie says with a laugh.

"It's a Design and Engineering Academy," I say. "Science is only part of it. And physics is actually my weakest subject."

"Excuse me." Sammie hates when I correct her, but it's like a tic that I can't control. "*A Design and Engineering Academy.*" She mocks me with a snotty pseudo-British accent.

"That sounds cool." Evan picks up my physics book and fans through it. "Did you, like, toss eggs from windows to understand their velocity?"

"Not at the Academy." I laugh. "But in my physics class, yes. With parachutes. But it was to understand resistance. I'm more into design theories." There I go correcting again, like a know-it-all, even though I'm more of a know-a-little-bit. I never really understood resistance all that well, and it's not like I could completely explain it if he asked.

But he doesn't even blink. "I'm more of a music man, myself, but I'm thinking about minoring in math. I love how it all connects. Geometry. Sequences. Chord patterns."

"You're in college?"

"Graduated last year, along with this blockhead." Evan throws a playful punch at Virgo. I find out that they're both enrolled at St. Mary's, a private university that's a few miles north.

Virgo punches him back. "Now we're roommates, and I've got to listen to Evan's god-awful singing."

Evan looks genuinely hurt. "Please don't tell my dad that you think my singing is god-awful," he says. "He already thinks I'm wasting my time as a music major. He doesn't need your professional opinion on my skills."

"Well, I really like your voice," Sammie says.

"Why, thank you!" He smiles at her. "See there, I've got at least one fan."

"Dude," Virgo says. "I was kidding."

"Evan also plays guitar," Sammie says to me. Right. I vaguely remember her gushing about these jam sessions they had last summer during the pool's closing on Saturday nights when it wasn't too crowded. She wanted me to come, but I never did. "Did you bring it?"

"Not today. Too many people." He puts down my book. "Were you planning on studying?"

"I didn't expect it to be this busy."

Some kids at the front of the line outside the gates whine for us to open. I look up at the clock. 8:58 A.M. "When do we let them in?"

"In exactly eighty-six seconds," Virgo says.

"Do we have to?" Evan complains.

"It's what we get paid to do."

"Well, I guess we should, then," Evan says, and then he turns to me and smiles. "It was nice to meet you, BFF."

I remember his peppermint lips on mine.

He's so very, very cute.

But I tell every cell in my body to resist. I've been burned before by friendly guys with nice smiles. I've made a promise to myself: no more relationships, no distractions, nothing until college. Or maybe even after.

No entanglements. No more trouble. Inertia. That's what you want, Viviana. Complete and utter inertia.

I slide my books under the counter, and Virgo takes out keys to open the gate. "I guess it's time. Here we go," he says. "Let summer begin."

"Well, Vivi"—Evan leans in and sings an unfamiliar melody in a voice deep and low and ever so enticing—"welcome to the madhouse."

College Admissions Tip #2

College admissions officers are definitely interested in what students do during summer breaks. They will not be swayed by empty holes in your time line. If you've done nothing more than hang around and goof off with friends instead of getting involved and showing leadership and growth, they will not be impressed.

There are just so many people, so many IDs. So much whining from the kids, so much eye rolling from the parents. It's rote and boring and constant.

Scan and check.

Scan and check.

I don't mention anything to Sammie about having met

Evan before. Her parents, protective as they were, didn't let her go to the party, and though I told her about kissing a random guy, there's no possible way she could know it was Evan.

"I'm waiting for my inertia," I say to Sammie.

"It's the first day. And it's hot, so everyone's here. It'll slow down in a week, when all the kids are in camp," she says. "Give it time."

The word *hot* doesn't even cut it. By 10:00 A.M., it's near ninety degrees, even though it's the end of May and technically still spring.

"It's not hot," I grumble. "It's a veritable hell."

"We'll get to go in the water soon, right?" Sammie says to Virgo as he works on the schedule behind us. "We'll get to swim?"

"Sure. On your days off," he says. "And during breaks, if you want."

Our lunch break isn't for another three hours, so that doesn't really help. It's only getting hotter by the minute. I guess the perks of semifree membership are supposed to keep us satisfied, but by midmorning, I'm sweating so hard, I'm ready to quit and tell my mom that she was right, that this is too much for me, that I'd rather spend all summer with Mila than sit in the heat and deal with crabby residents who yell at us when we can't fully explain why their passes from last summer are invalid or their whiny kids who cry because the snack bar doesn't carry Kit Kats.

"Forget inertia," I say to Sammie. "Didn't you promise me 'awesome'?"

Sammie rolls her eyes.

But then, something interesting happens. Not awesome. But interesting. Entertaining, at the very least.

The Nut arrives.

There he stands—the man who lives a few floors below me with his nervous Chihuahua and self-portraits—in front of us, chewing gum, snapping it loudly. When I ask him to sign a form sent from the association for all first-time swimmers, he grumbles at me. "I gotta use a black pen? Goddamn Mercury retrograde—it's a bitch."

After we check his ID and finish scanning him in, Sammie reads his form. "Harold Joseph Cox?" she says. "That *cannot* be his real name. Let's hope he doesn't ever go by Harry."

I can't help but giggle. "Not much better than 'the Nut.' Poor guy. That is quite unfortunate."

"I'm a nut, I'm a nut, a nut, nut, nut," she sings under her breath.

"Stop," I say. "Be nice."

We lean over the counter to watch him. He's bone-thin, and his skin is like leather. He throws his towel onto an empty chair, dives headfirst into the deep end, and swims the length of the pool underwater until his bald head pops up in the far shallow end. Then he jumps out of the water, grabs his towel, and whisks right past us without saying good-bye or anything.

"Well, that was a short swim," I say.

Sammie laughs.

And that's that.

Or so we think.

Because then twenty minutes later, he comes back. He's completely dry and in a new bathing suit—a red one in place of the black one before.

He walks to the edge of the pool, dives in, swims just like he did before, pops out of the water, grabs his towel, and leaves.

"Um. Okay, freak," Sammie says.

Another half hour goes by, and he appears, dry and in *another* new bathing suit—this one blue. We scan his card. He dives in. He swims. He leaves.

"That's weird, right?" Sammie asks.

"Yeah. That's weird."

He repeats this routine three more times before our break at 1:00 P.M.

Arrives in a new, dry bathing suit (yellow). Dives in. Leaves.

Arrives in another new, dry bathing suit (white). Dives in. Leaves.

Six times in two hours.

"What the hell?" Sammie says. "How many bathing suits does he own?"

Virgo reminds us to take our break. The pool is too packed to swim and we're starving, so we run down the street to Rocket Subs, where we split a twelve-inch veggie with extra pickles. We could easily have gone up to either of our apartments for leftovers, but we want some semblance of a summer.

When we get back an hour later, Virgo and Vanessa are sitting in for us at the front desk, playing with their phones.

It's calmed down. There's no line and a lot of the families have left for the afternoon.

"You're back!" Virgo says. He looks straight at me. "Your friend came looking for you."

"Our friend?" Sammie asks.

"Harold Cox?" Virgo reads the log. "The guy who was here like ten times this morning?"

"Six," I say.

Virgo and Vanessa stand up to give us our chairs back.

"I didn't know you were counting."

"Yeah, well," Vanessa says before she leaves us to relieve Evan from his chair. "He was here. He got in line, and we were about to scan his card, but when he saw it was us, he turned around and went back upstairs."

"It's like he's waiting for you guys," Virgo says. "Like he's just here for *you*."

"Shut up. Gross!" Sammie says. "No thanks. There's no way I want the Nut waiting for us."

Evan approaches from the deck. "The Nut? Who are you talking about?"

"You know. Your friend," Virgo says. "Mr. Harry Cox."

I can't help but laugh. I mean, it is a terrible name.

"Professor Cox is a great guy," Evan says earnestly.

"*Professor* Cox?" Sammie asks.

"He teaches psychology at St. Mary's. I met him here last year and we talked for hours. He's fascinating. Won't tell you a thing about himself, but he'll discuss the effect of neurochemistry on interpersonal relationships, ideas like love maps and the triangular theory of love for hours and hours, if you have time. I don't even need another psych class on my schedule after finishing 101, but I signed up for social psychology with him anyway in the fall."

"The triangular theory of love?" I ask.

"Intimacy, passion, and commitment," Evan recites. "The three essential components of love, according to one theorist."

"What was up with his little parade of Speedos this morning?" Sammie asks.

"I don't know. I saw that. And he didn't say a word to me all morning. It was like he didn't remember me at all," Evan says. "Why do you call him 'the Nut'?"

"It's what Vivi's little sister calls him," Sammie says, and then she makes me tell them the story about the pistachios, and we sing two verses and the chorus of the "I'm a Nut" song.

He gives us a *guess you had to be there* look, and I suddenly feel like a child for making fun of someone who probably suffers with issues. "Sorry," I say finally. "Do you think he has a mental disorder?"

"Honestly, I don't think so," Evan says. "He's incredibly intelligent. Sure, he exhibits some behaviors, as he himself might describe, that fall outside of the normative, but he can't help it. It's probably his own little game, some experiment he's conducting to test our reactions. He's probably the one doing the observing."

God, I like Evan. Besides the hotness factor, I like how he talks, how he thinks. I like that he's smart and sharp and—I don't know—open to possibility.

Evan's smiling. "Hey, you guys. I just thought of something. Do you want to play a game?"

"Oh no," Virgo says. "Not a game."

Sammie explains. "Each summer involves some kind of game."

"Usually it's just a bet," Evan says. "Like how many banana hammocks in one day. Or how long until a kid throws up."

"Banana hammocks?" I ask.

"Speedos," Sammie explains.

"Nothing too serious," Evan insists. "No one will get hurt or anything like that."

"Well, except last summer," Virgo says, *"someone"*—he looks at Evan—"stole the stamp from Rocket Subs and a bunch of those 'Buy eight, eat one free' cards. They tallied how many free subs they could get before the owner realized and got a new stamp."

"Sixteen days, twenty-two subs," Evan says with pride.

"Yeah, and that didn't end well," Virgo says. "Jasmine Picard almost got fired for that little escapade, since she was the one in charge. And now you're on my watch."

"Walk away if you're not interested," Evan says. "Bennett pool games are a long-standing tradition, one that cannot be stalled by one minor unfortunate conclusion."

Virgo takes his advice and walks away.

Evan opens a locker on the wall behind us, pulls out his wallet, and then jumps up and sits on the counter, right next to me. "Are you betting girls?"

His face is lit with excitement, and I answer quickly. "Depends," I say. "I could be a betting girl."

Something about him strikes something in me—maybe it's the lame memory of my fifteen seconds in heaven—but

I instantly regret my response. I am not a betting girl. I am a play-by-the-rules, don't-ever-get-in-trouble girl. I mean, I used to be. Once should have been enough to teach me a good lesson.

And then Sammie kicks me under the counter.

"Ouch."

I look at her. *He's mine,* her eyes say.

She's into him. I hadn't realized. Of course. Why wouldn't she be? He's cute. He's smart. He's funny.

My friendship with Sammie matters more than anything, except Mila. And anyway, the last thing I need right now is the distraction of a cute, smart, and funny guy. Her kick forces me to recall my promise—to myself, to my family—to keep it all together.

But before I can back out, Evan smiles at me and says, "Excellent." And then he turns to Sammie. "What about you? Play with us?"

She pulls out her wallet, even though I know money's tight for her. "Of course I'm in. What are we betting on?"

"Simple. What time he'll come back. Two bucks each. The one closest to the real time wins the pot." He puts his money on the counter. "But we need to round up more players."

Evan leaves us to invite the other guards to join the pot, and Sammie collapses onto the counter.

"Why are you kicking me? Do you like him?"

"Ugh," she mumbles. "It doesn't matter. It's obvious he's into you."

"No thanks," I say, lying to myself and to her. "You know I've sworn off guys forever."

She lifts her head. "Oh come on, Vivi, forever? Just because of one minor incident?"

"No," I remind her. "Just because of one major scandal involving one major jerkwad who ruined my reputation for life."

"What reputation? Here at Bennett Tower Pool, there is no scandal. You have no reputation. No one here knows anything about you."

"Seriously. You should totally go for Evan," I say.

"But—"

"Really. I'm not interested. At all. He's all yours. I just want to take it easy this summer, use my time to get back on track in school, and enjoy not knowing anyone."

"Excellent." She leans over the counter and kisses me on the cheek. "Let the flirting commence."

Evan returns to the counter. "We've got a pretty decent pot going. Virgo's sitting out, but everyone else is in."

"I'm in, too," I say, and I pull the money from my wallet. "Two bucks each, right?"

"Yes!" Evan yells. "She's in!"

And so it begins.

This silly game and our wait for Professor Cox to return.

The job isn't quite awesome yet, but it's interesting, at the very least. Much better than the McDonald's alternative. I'm surrounded by people who aren't judging me on my past or scrutinizing my future life goals.

Evan puts his hand on my shoulder and squeezes tight. "We have a game!"

His hand rests there for a good long moment. I don't want him to let go.

Sammie kicks me again.

I shrug off Evan's hand and try to send a psychic message back: *He's all yours. I don't want any more trouble. I want to do right by you and everyone else in my life. I just want to be good again.*

College Admissions Tip #3

College admissions boards seek well-rounded students who show an investment in a sport or an activity where you have learned something, developed a skill, and perhaps even contributed to the group in new and meaningful ways.

I win the first round after guessing that Professor Cox will return in twenty-nine minutes, which is only one minute off from when he actually returns. I win eight bucks, and Evan sends me the happiest smile. "Aren't you glad you decided to play?"

I don't answer. I refuse to flirt back.

Marquis and Vanessa join in on the second round, and Marquis wins. Thirty-four minutes, three minutes off. He wins fourteen bucks. The others are down four.

Evan finally throws Sammie a thumbs-up from his post on deck when Professor Cox arrives thirty-one minutes later, which she guesses right on the dot.

Professor Cox repeats his pool-dip routine six times after that.

Just as the sun starts to duck behind the Bennett Tower, we've each won one round, except for Evan and Sammie, who have both won two. Of course, she's incredibly pleased.

Each time Professor Cox comes down, he's in a new bathing suit.

Once, while Evan is hanging out in the office, he attempts conversation with him—"Hey, Professor Cox, are you teaching summer classes?"—but Professor Cox ignores him.

Each time, there's no eye contact, no interaction.

But then, on what is the twelfth time that day (twenty-eight minutes, my win), Professor Cox talks to us.

Well, not really to us, more like to himself, or to no one in particular.

That seems to break the seal on his weirdness. I swear I hear him say "Didya ever eat a wallaby? Tasty little suckers." And then he breaks into a hoarse fit of hysterics, his bony, bare shoulders pumping up and down.

Evan isn't here to hear it, and I'm wondering about all those fascinating conversations he had with him last year.

Professor Cox does his thing and then leaves.

Sammie takes two more dollars from her wad of cash and slams it on the counter. "I say twenty-eight minutes until he returns."

Our shift ends at four, but we stay so that we can continue playing. I don't want the stupid game to end, and I don't want to work at McDonald's. I want to be here, sweating in this cabana/office, next to my best friend, placing stupid bets on an odd man. It's going to be a long, hot summer, but I like feeling like I belong to a group of people who accept me just as I am, even if they don't really know me at all.

"Only eighteen minutes until closing," Vanessa says. "There's no way he's coming down again."

"Oh, he's coming," Evan says. "Put your money down, people! The final bet of the day is about to close!"

The pool has pretty much cleared out. It's near 7:00 P.M. and most of the families are gone, having showered and packed up. All the lifeguards, except for Virgo, who's on duty in his chair, are gathered around us in the office.

"He's not coming!" Vanessa laughs. "Marquis, do you really think he's coming?"

"I doubt it, but I don't want to give up hope, either. I'll say twelve minutes."

"I call sixteen minutes," Virgo yells from the deck. He's finally succumbed to the lure of the game. "He'll be here!"

"I'm with Virgo," I say. "He's going to be here. Put down fourteen minutes for me. But I'm raising the stakes. I'm putting in ten."

Evan laughs. "Baller! Ten bucks! I'm in!"

Vanessa steps back. "I need the money for gas. I'm out."

Marquis throws a ten-dollar bill into the pile. "I'm in."

"Ten?" Sammie snaps a sharp look at me. "I can't do ten—" Sammie's family struggles even more with money than mine. Her mom inherited their apartment from her family, but that was before Sammie's dad died. Sammie's mom, a nurse, is always taking extra shifts to make ends meet.

"You don't have to place a bet," I whisper. "Vanessa's out. You can sit this one out, too."

She looks at Evan, and then takes a deep breath. "Fine."

"What if he doesn't show up?" Vanessa asks.

"We all get our money back," Evan says.

"Then I hope he doesn't show up," Sammie whispers to me.

There are only fifteen minutes to go.

Sammie is the winner.

At nine minutes before closing, Professor Cox arrives, this time wearing a thick black robe.

"Oh, thank God," Sammie mutters under her breath.

I take Professor Cox's ID card and scan him in.

He signs his name.

I wait for him to say something.

But he doesn't.

He just walks in.

Evan walks over to the pool to test the pH of the water. Sammie and I step out of our little room to watch. We wait for Professor Cox to throw off his robe. To walk down to the deep end. To dive in. To do his thing.

But instead, he heads to the shallow end.

He takes off his robe and jumps in.

But this time it's feet first.

And this time it's delicate, deliberate, slow.

His back is to Virgo, and he's hunched over, like he's holding his stomach.

I can see the splashing, and I can hear some strange moaning, but I can't really figure out what it is.

Then, I hear it—the barking and yelping—and Virgo is jumping out of his chair, running toward Professor Cox. "Hey! No dogs! Come out of the pool, please! Now!"

It's Professor Cox's Chihuahua, paddling around in dog-size goggles and red swimming trunks that match Professor Cox's.

At first, Professor Cox ignores Virgo, just lets his Chihuahua swim into the deep end, past the few remaining old women, who start yelping right along with the dog.

Evan drops his pH gear and runs over. He's crouching down and yelling out, but Professor Cox doesn't respond.

Finally, Professor Cox catches the dog, climbs out without saying a word to either Virgo or Evan. He throws on his robe and treks past us and back upstairs, that poor creature dripping and shivering under his arm.

After they calm the old ladies and clear out the pool for final closing, Evan and Virgo come back to the office.

"Nice going, Viviana." Evan gives me a very serious look. "First day on the job and you're already letting wild animals into the water."

My heart drops. "Oh God, I'm so sorry. Am I in trouble?" I don't want to be fired on my very first day. My mom would kill me.

"No." Virgo laughs. "You're not in trouble."

Evan's face changes to a smile. "Come on. I was just kidding."

I feel bad, though. I like making trouble, but I don't like being in trouble. "Okay, but really, I'm sorry. I promise I'll pay better attention next time."

Virgo laughs. "You've got to stop apologizing so much."

And then Evan puts his hand on my shoulder, and every muscle in my body melts. "Come on, it's funny."

I force out a laugh. "Yeah," I say. "Real funny."

He's right. It's nothing. It's a dog. It's silliness and stupidity.

But then I catch Sammie's sad stare. She's focusing on Evan's hand on me. She's not laughing. She's not having a good time.

I quickly shrug off his shoulder. "Yeah. Okay. You're right. I'm fine. It's nothing."

It may just be silliness and stupidity to him, but if I'm not careful, it could turn into another fine mess.

During dinner, I tell Mila and my mom the story of Professor Cox and his dog, which makes Mila giggle with that deep belly laugh I love.

My mom doesn't laugh. She just shakes her head. "I know who you're talking about," she says. "Harold. I know him."

"You *know* him?" Mila and I yell in unison.

"Not personally. He and I have only exchanged a few words. Sammie's mom knows him better. I've seen them talking to each other."

"About what?"

"I couldn't say. I have no idea." But the way she says it makes me think she does, and whatever it is about, she doesn't approve.

Mila takes a guess. "Maybe they're secretly in love with each other and are going to get married!"

"Doubtful." I laugh.

I grab my phone from the kitchen counter and text Sammie. *Your mom knows Professor Cox. Ask him about his—*

But before I can finish my text, my mom snaps at me. "What is that thing doing at the dinner table?"

She's talking about my phone. Ever since the Dean incident, she's become the enemy of all devices, particularly if I'm near any. After some deep negotiations, we finally agreed that I could keep my computer for schoolwork and that I could have a cheap twenty-dollar replacement phone that takes only calls and texts—no apps, no online photos. My mom adds minutes each month and checks my usage, but at least she didn't completely cut off my lifeline to the world.

I don't answer her. I just slide my phone back on the counter and take a bite of my chicken.

Mila slides down into her chair. "Can we please have one night when we don't argue?" She looks like she's going to cry.

I reach over for her hand and look at my mom. My mom keeps her eyes down at her plate, ignores Mila's question.

I smile at my sister. "Yes. No problem. One night with no arguments. We can totally do that."

My mom still doesn't say anything.

I squeeze Mila's hand and take a sip of water.

We continue eating in silence. No more stories, no more belly laughs. Mila's question hangs in the air. We're not arguing, but we're not talking, either.

College Essay Tip

Be yourself in your essay. It's important to be both honest and specific so that the readers can "hear" your voice. The essay is an opportunity for you to humanize your otherwise-sterile application. Telling your unique story allows you to stand out!

Viviana Rabinovich-Lowe
Common Application
Very Rough Draft #1

Prompt: Write about someone who has had an impact on you.

They say to pour everything into a rough draft and then edit for what's essential later. So here it is: I choose my very best friend, Samantha Lailani Gabriela Salazar, aka

Sammie, as the single most important human being on this earth.

Why Sammie? First, she knows almost everything about me. We've been friends since before kindergarten, partly since we live so close to each other and our moms were friends first. You might say proximity forced us together, but we've never resented it.

It is true that we're very different. Even in elementary school, I was shy and quiet and my teachers loved me. Sammie, on the other hand, was loud and bold and was always getting yellow and red cards for talking during class. But she made me giggle, and I can't remember a day when we weren't together. When I was with her, I wasn't shy anymore. When I was with her, I could be myself. When I was with her, I laughed.

By the time we got to middle school, there were some times I felt like I could hardly keep up with her inspired schemes. She ran barefoot in the snow. She cooked small pieces of aluminum foil in her aunt's microwave to watch the fires ignite. She once downed two cans of Coca-Cola in under two minutes and then proceeded to burp the entire "Star-Spangled Banner" for my amusement alone. We were polar opposites, but she still kept me around, maybe because I laughed.

She's also brilliant. I mean, her dad was an English teacher at our high school. And, thanks to him, we both love to read, and that's part of what we can spend hours bonding over. It's part of what I love about her.

I've always looked up to Sammie and was especially in awe of her ability to flirt. We both developed at the same time, earlier than the other girls in our class. At that time,

I felt incredibly self-conscious about my broad shoulders and large chest, my thick hips and thighs, which never fit into any pants at places like Urban Outfitters. Sammie and I are built similarly, and she says it's because "we come from people who love to eat." But it never seemed to bother her that we're substantially bigger than the other girls, and so eventually she taught me to feel the same. She's also photogenic, with a heart-shaped face and thick black hair that cascades down her back. She's mastered the art of the selfie. She's figured out how to shop. She likes clothes. Clothes like her.

So, I was sure she'd be the one to get a boyfriend first. We both were.

When we got to high school, she made lists of the guys she thought were cute, while I made lists of colleges, with help from my dad. Not just one list. Lists. It didn't matter what year they were, how old they were, if they were athletic or dorky, some brooding senior, full of angst, or some scrawny freshman who smiled nicely. She flirted with them all. And they all seemed to want to flirt back.

But I don't know. Nothing ever happened. She went out on a few dates, but nothing ever stuck. Maybe it's because her dad was a teacher at our school, and they were too afraid to go for her.

You can imagine our mutual shock when Dean and I got together.

"So that's why you take all these ridiculously hard classes?" she said when I called her up to tell her the news. "So you can hook up with other nerds?"

"No. It's so I can learn more and get into a good college."

"Where you'll undoubtedly hook up with more nerds, marry one glorious supernerd, and then proceed to have cute little nerd babies."

"You know, you're a supernerd, too, or you wouldn't be at Uni."

"Thanks, but you know I'm at Uni because of my dad." Uni Lab High is a college prep school associated with the local university, and you have to pass a test to get in.

"That's not true, so stop it," I said. "Anyway, don't doom me to a future of matrimony, old age, and death. Maybe I don't want to get married. Maybe I want to live on my own, be by myself, do my own thing. Maybe I don't want to have kids." I thought about my sister, how much work she was when she was a baby, and how I've already helped raise one.

"Maybe you want to grow old alone, surrounded by dozens of feral cats?"

"Yes," I said. "Maybe."

"Just promise me you'll always love me, even though I'll never be as smart as you."

"Stop saying you're not smart." I hate it when she puts herself down. Sammie's one of the smartest, funniest people I know, but she likes to do this self-deprecating thing, and it makes me crazy.

"Just say you'll love me forever," she said. "And that you'll let me be the godmother to your cute little nerd babies."

"You know I'll love you forever. And if I choose not to have babies, you can help me take care of my twenty-six cats."

"I'm not scooping the crap of twenty-six cats out of your litter boxes."

"That's okay," I said. "I'll love you anyway. I'll always love you, Sammie."

And I always will.

She's the only one who didn't judge me when my ex-boyfriend spread that photo of me around school. Once upon a time, I had a decent supply of friends. Sammie had always been my true one and only, but we also were open to being social with the other kids in our class. Uni High is relatively small, so a scandal like the one I got myself into is big news.

The day I returned from winter break was bad. I walked into side eyes and murmurs and muffled laughter from the very same people who I'd previously called my friends. It was like there was this new invisible cloud around me, one that kept people from actually talking to me, but one that made them want to stare, as though I was an F-up, a sideshow freak. It was as though, by staring, they could make me do it again. They'd already seen a part of me—my body—in the picture, and I could feel their eyes, not looking at my face to see if I was still a person, but looking at my clothes, trying to see through them, trying to see me naked again.

I found notes in my locker, on my desk, in my bag, sometimes just words like "cyberslut" or "photo whore" or "sext skank." But there were also those trying to be clever: "Congrats, you have won Uni's Distinguished Award of Resident A+ Slut."

Each one was a punch to my gut.

Each one was a reminder of how badly I'd messed up.

Sammie stayed by my side and told me to ignore them. "Don't let them get to you. They want you to lose control. Just don't let them."

I tried, really hard, to focus on the lecture or on my homework or on the hallway floor or her hand tight around my elbow, but there was no ignoring the reality that I was a complete failure.

My dad had his one-way ticket to Singapore, and my mom wouldn't talk to me about any of it—not his leaving, not the separation, not my new status as resident Uni "slut." She'd just give me these sad, judgmental looks. It was bad enough I had to deal with the piercing stares at school, but I got to come home to more from my own mother.

During a wholly uncomfortable meeting with her, Ms. McKee, the principal, and Ms. Fuentes, the counselor, they said that I should report any bullying immediately, and they promised that they were there for me, whatever I needed. But then, at the end of the week, they held a special assembly with the entire school to discuss the realities of bullying and to teach lessons on compassion and kindness. They defined the differences between psychological bullying and physical bullying, giving lists of examples of each. They gave warnings about suspensions and expulsions. It was supposed to be this general assembly, not in relation to anyone in particular, they said, but then they spent all this time telling stories of kids who had killed themselves from the pressure of "cyberbullying and sexting incidents," and, of course, everyone in the auditorium looked at me.

I tried to keep my head up high, like Sammie told me to. I tried not to slide down into my seat. I tried to hold back the tears. I felt her squeeze my hand, and so I chanted to myself: Do not lose control. Do not lose control. Do not lose control.

But the reality was, if there was anyone who didn't know about the photo before, they certainly sought it out after the assembly. There was no way to erase all of the copies online. They had been shared and retweeted and retumbled and reblogged. They were there. For good.

That's when I had the first Episode.

Ms. McKee and Ms. Fuentes had just opened the room to Q & A when some jackass freshman, Jared Wentz, two rows behind me, whispered my name, and without thinking, I turned around. He flashed his phone at me, and there it was: me, naked, in his creepy little hands. I turned back in my seat, my jaw clenched, my heart racing. I slid into my seat.

Sammie turned around and snapped at the kid: "Shut that off right now." A bunch of kids laughed around us until a teacher came over and shushed them.

No one had any questions for Ms. McKee and Ms. Fuentes, so they ended the assembly and told us to go back to our regular schedule. Sammie had to go to math, while I had to go to physics, so she hugged me and whispered in my ear: "Don't let them get to you. I'm sure they've all sent their own pics, but they were just lucky enough not to get caught."

I let go of her and made my way toward lab, wishing she were next to me to defend me from all the vicious stares and murmurs. I chanted again: Do not lose control. Do not lose control. Do not lose control.

That's when I heard it. Jared Wentz. He was following

me now, calling out to me again, but this time, he was moaning my name.

"Viviaaaaaana."

He was repeating my name, and then breathing heavily, in a sexual way, moaning and groaning and grunting at me.

"Viviaaaaaana."

The kids around us laughed, which only served to encourage him.

"Viviaaaaaana."

I vaguely remember stopping.

I vaguely remember trying to tell him to stop.

I vaguely remember the spinning hallway, the echoes of laughter, other kids joining in, moaning and groaning around me.

And then I remember—clearly—Sammie. She appeared as though from nowhere. She yelled at them, all of them, called them names, told them to get away from me.

She held my arm, led me to the bathroom, where I collapsed on the cold tile floor.

"I. Can't. Breathe."

I vaguely remember the body spasms, the hot flashes of terror in my chest, the floor like a sinkhole. I could have melted into it.

I could have lost complete control.

But she didn't let me. Instead, she held me, patted wet paper towels against my forehead. She rubbed my back. She sat with me for an hour, until I was able to breathe again, and then she snuck me out of the building, led me to a park down the street, where she lay with me in the grass and told me to cry.

The next day, her math teacher called her up to the front of the room and chided her, in front of everyone, about cutting class. Sammie walked out and went straight to Ms. McKee, telling her about Jared and what he'd done to me.

The news of my promiscuity was quickly replaced by the news of Jared's expulsion, and thereafter, the stares stopped. It turns out that for Uni nerds, the fear of banishment is more powerful than the thrill of a good scandal. Sometimes I still find printed copies of the photo deposited anonymously in my locker or I'll hear whispers behind me, but considering how bad it was, I've survived the rest of the semester with relative ease. And I have Sammie to directly thank for that.

College Admissions Tip #4

REMINDER: Junior Year Grades Are Essential!

These grades are the last that the admissions boards will see, and they can determine your college fate. They show that you're ready for the big time. This is your best chance to impress!

Sammie and I still have to endure the torture of school for another two weeks, but since the APs and Sammie's play are over (she had the lead role, of course, of Abigail in *The Crucible*), we're scheduled to work afternoons until school's out, when we'll be able to work mornings, too. By our shift Tuesday afternoon, the pool is nearly deserted, just as Sammie predicted.

The afternoon is quiet and lazy, which is good, because

I need the time to study for finals, even with the nausea and dizziness that come and go in waves, which I tell no one about. The only productive thing I can really do, other than leave town from the public shaming, is focus on getting through it without completely bombing all my classes.

Sammie's reading horoscopes on her phone, and as much as I try to remind her that I need to study, she continues to interrupt me with forecasts regarding my health and career over the next year.

About twenty minutes before closing, Evan approaches from the deck. He sits down on the counter and hovers over us. "Whatcha reading?"

Sammie lights up. "What's your sign? Wait—let me guess. Scorpio?"

"I have no idea. March twenty-ninth?"

"Aries. Of course. I totally see that."

"How, exactly, do you see that?"

"Aries are, like, pure energy, confident and adventurous. I see that in you."

"Well, thanks," he says, and then he pokes at my book. "What's your sign, Vivi?"

Ugh. Please don't do this. Talk to Sammie instead.

I ignore him long enough that Sammie answers for me. "She's a moody Cancer. I'm a Leo. Aries and Leos have a high affinity. Did you know that?" She doesn't say that Cancers and Aries have the lowest compatibility possible on the zodiac, but I know she wants to.

"You really believe this stuff?" Evan asks. "I mean, it can't really predict the future, so why bother reading it?"

"You'd be surprised! I usually read it at the end of the

day to see if it was right, and more often than not, it is. A lot of our energy is written in the movement of the planets."

"But what about for people who get really sick or die? It never says, 'When Neptune passes the fourth moon of Pluto this Tuesday at noon, avoid walking under cranes or you'll be a flattened mess of blood and bones.'"

"Of course not. But it might say that it's a good time to stay home and curl up on the couch with a good book."

"When isn't it a good time to curl up with a good book?" He laughs and turns to me. Again. "Are you also reading about the mystical secrets of planetary alignments?"

I lift up my physics textbook and shake my head no. I don't want to get into a conversation with him. I want him to focus on Sammie, not me. At least, that's what I remind myself.

Evan leans over my book. "Does science have anything to say about Saturn's impact on human destiny?"

I can't help but laugh, but this makes Sammie frown.

I'm about to say that I think it's fun anyway, when Professor Cox walks up to sign out. "What do you want to know about human destiny?" He's shivering and shaking, dripping wet, and standing less then two feet away, but he yells this as though he's lecturing in a classroom.

"Hey, Professor," Evan says. "Perfect timing! Here's the question of the day. Horoscopes: yea or nay?"

Professor Cox lifts his towel to wipe his forehead. "If you're asking if it's possible to change the future, there is no scientific evidence, of course."

"My point exactly!" Evan says. "It's a waste of time. It doesn't actually *do* anything."

Sammie clicks off her phone and stuffs it in her bag.

"Wait a minute," I say. "Why does it bother you so much? If we read our horoscopes or not?"

Evan puts his hands up. "Whoa. I'm sorry. I was just kidding—"

"Seriously, though. If it makes Sammie feel better about her day, why do you care? Why is it such an issue for you?"

"Actually," Professor Cox says, "she's right. Horoscopes do serve as a valid cognitive trick, like hindsight bias, and they can help us navigate rough times. We invoke the idea of fate via activities like astrology in order to reflect upon and accept the reality of our situations, the choices we've already made."

"Exactly," I continue. "Thank you. And therefore I am in full support of Sammie reading her horoscope if it means she'll feel better about those choices."

"Okay, okay—" Evan puts up his hands and smiles at me. "It all makes sense now." And then he puts his hand on my shoulder, squeezes me tight. "That's a perfect argument."

Sammie stands up. "I'm out." She straps her bag over her shoulder. "See you guys tomorrow."

I was trying to defend her, but now I've stepped into the spotlight, and she's pissed.

"Wait. Where are you going?" I ask. There's still ten minutes before closing.

She doesn't answer, though. Instead, she walks out the door without clocking out. She does this sometimes, turns off at a moment's notice.

Evan looks confused, but I don't wait to explain. "I'm going to head out, too," I say.

I clock out quickly for both Sammie and me, and then I grab my bag and try to catch up with her. I run through the courtyard, but she's out of sight. I struggle to find my key to the back entrance door of our building. By the time I get to the elevator, she's already disappeared.

She's ignoring my texts. I run upstairs and knock on her door, but Mrs. Salazar answers and says that Sammie's locked herself in her room, that she might be taking a nap. I hate it when she does this. She shuts off, shuts me out. It's the only thing about having a best friend who's a drama geek that drives me crazy. She reads into everything.

Admittedly, this time, she's right. Evan was showing interest only in me. I felt it. She felt it. We both felt it.

And maybe if it weren't for Sammie, I might be interested, too. The more I'm around him, the more I like him. I'm not sure why exactly. Maybe because he asks questions that make me step outside of myself, away from my wandering, hurting mind.

But I've made a promise to her.

I've made a promise to myself.

I head back down to my apartment, where Mila is zoned out on the couch, watching her animal show, and my mom is in the dining room, on her computer, like always, studying for her class.

I try to get to my room without her noticing me, but of course that's impossible in this tiny apartment. "You were late today," she says. "I thought the pool closed at seven, no?"

"It did. It does. I was just helping them clean up."

"Do they pay you for that?"

"Yeah, actually," I say, lying. "Mr. Bautista said I could work overtime."

"There are laws in Illinois that govern how many hours minors can work each week. He'd better not be breaking them."

"Oh. I didn't know that." Whoops. Just my luck that my mom, with her photographic memory, has probably memorized the entire Illinois legal library.

"I thought this was going to be an easy job. And that you were going to be home on time." She says this as a statement, not a question. She doesn't ask how it's going, if I even like it. She just assumes that I'm doing something wrong.

"It is an easy job," I say. "I was just having fun. I wanted to stay a little longer, that's all."

This somehow appeases her, for now. "You go lie down now."

I don't tell her that I don't want to lie down. Or that I have finals to study for. Or that I'm tired of her telling me what to do instead of asking me how I am.

I head to my room and shut the door.

The next morning, I wake up to five texts from Sammie. She's read all my texts, heard my voice mails, accepted my apology. She knows it's not my fault—it's just that she thought she liked him so much, and it's totally fine if I want to go for him—she'll never be one to get in the way of true love.

I call her up.

"I'm telling you. I'm not into him."

"But it's okay if you are." She's using her drama voice again, the one that's too high-pitched to be real.

"I'm not, though." Despite whatever force I felt draw me toward him, the last thing I need right now is to be dating anyone. "Anyway, he was being kind of a jerk to you, with that whole horoscope thing."

"I think he was just trying to get your attention. He liked it when you stood up for me."

"Let's just drop it. Okay?"

"You're sure?" she asks. "I can go for him, and you're one hundred percent totally okay with it."

"Yes. Absolutely. I'm one hundred and *fifty* percent totally okay with it," I say. "Would you please stop asking me? I'll see you downstairs in ten minutes?"

"Okay, fine. Yes. Sure. See you downstairs."

We make our way to school. Our teachers are frantic about cramming everything in before finals week, while we're all feeling exhausted and done. I'm especially ready for the year to be over, for all the silent, judgmental stares and snickers to stop.

Sammie and I arrive at the pool for our afternoon shift, to find Evan sitting behind the front desk in our usual place, the most serious expression on his face. Professor Cox's there, too, sitting on the counter, next to him. They're so deep in conversation, they don't even notice us.

"I don't know, Professor Cox," Evan's saying. "I have to disagree with you. True love is absolutely possible. It happens every day." It's as though they've been here since yesterday, waxing philosophical about the meaning of life.

"Well, sure, if you want to call infatuation and disappointment 'love.' You can give it any name you like," Professor Cox says. "But it's an arbitrary word for an artificial experience that's temporary, at best. As Fromm says, love 'is not a sentiment which can be easily indulged in by anyone. One cannot fall in love. One has to be in love.' With oneself. With others. With life. But that kind of love is nearly impossible."

Evan stands up to give us our seats at the desk and then jumps over the front of the counter, where they continue their conversation without acknowledging our arrival.

"You really believe that, Professor Cox? That it's arbitrary? That it's impossible? You don't believe that there's some kind of universal feeling or knowing or whatever you want to call it—one that becomes embodied in our individual experiences—and then, when it's shared by two people, it's understood by both beings as a remembrance of what is true about this world?"

"Shared by two people. Ha! You are limiting yourself, Mr. Whitlock!" Professor Cox laughs and then continues: "But I admire that you're a true romantic, Mr. Whitlock. A visionary of the highest Victorian ideals."

"Why are you so disillusioned, Professor Cox?"

"I've lived a very full life, Evan. That's why." And then he says, more quietly, "It's been a very full and very long life."

Evan disregards this last, depressing comment and finally looks at us to back him up. "What do you guys think?"

"About the possibility of love?" Sammie asks.

"*True* love," Evan says. "Not just like love as a real force in the world but the love between two human beings, a love that is both romantic and eternal, something more than just an empty promise."

If swooning was still a thing that happened, if women really still fainted when overcome with emotion, if it could be heard and seen like a burning candle, Sammie would be a hot puddle of wax on the floor.

Except that then Evan leans back over the counter, so that he's hovering over me. I'm not sure if Sammie notices this, but I sure do.

"Of course," Sammie says. "I completely believe it. My mom and dad loved each other—I mean, until he died."

"Oh, I'm sorry," Evan says. "I didn't know."

"No, it's fine." Her voice cracks a little. "I mean, it's been a year since he died, but I know my mom still loves him, and I know he still loves her, wherever he is. It's eternal. No question." I reach out and wrap my pinkie around hers, squeeze it tight. She squeezes back.

We were at the end of sophomore year when Mr. Salazar died. He first became sick the same time as my mom, when Sammie and I were in the ninth grade. For a while, my mom was worse than Sammie's dad. My mom had cancer, whereas her dad had some heart problems that were supposed to be easily fixed with a simple procedure and a change in diet. And then, right after my mom went in for her last round of iodine treatment, Mr. Salazar was dead.

Sammie likes to say that her parents shared a love that

is as close to true love as will ever be seen on this earth. Her dad was such a good man. I remember how he would play dolls with us and then let us dress him in bows and makeup. I remember him teasing my mom, trying to convince her that her homemade kugel tasted better than Filipino banana sauce. I remember how much he and my dad liked each other; he'd try to talk to my dad about the NFL draft, but when he realized my dad had nothing to offer, he'd easily change the topic to the redevelopment of the West Side industrial neighborhoods and urban congestion, and they'd end up talking for hours. Most of all, I remember how good he was to Sammie's mom, how he'd always tell Sammie's mom to lie down instead of do the dishes because she'd been up all night with her patients. I remember how he recited Shakespearean sonnets to Sammie's mom on her birthday. I remember how he'd massage her shoulders and tell her he loved her.

Sammie doesn't say it because he's dead. She's not just sentimental. They really did love each other.

"My parents have been together for forty-seven years, since they were seventeen," Evan says. "And they're still in love with each other."

"Wow, is that even possible?" I ask. "How old are they?"

"They're sixty-four. My mom was forty-five when she had me. I was a 'miracle baby,' they said."

"That's amazing," Sammie says. "That your parents are so much older, I mean."

"Well, my dad had a minor stroke last year, though, and he's been struggling with his health ever since. I was originally going to take a year off after high school to backpack around Europe, and then my plan was to move to San Francisco and go to a music school where I applied and was accepted. They said I would have been able to defer enrollment. But my dad, an accountant, hated the idea. We had this big fight, and then that night, he threw a clot." This sort of pours out of him, and he says it all without any real emotion, like it was just a thing that happened.

Professor Cox cackles. "So you stayed home because of a guilt trip?"

Evan nods. "Yup. Pretty much."

"Well, it's a fact that we're all waiting for our parents to die so that we can finally live how we want."

"That's a terrible thing to say," Sammie says.

"It may be terrible," Professor Cox says, "but it's the truth."

This breaks Evan's quiet contemplation, and he laughs. "Professor Cox is known for his hard truths. It's why he makes the big bucks." Then he looks at me. "What about you?"

"Me?"

"Yes, you."

"What about me?"

"Love. True love. Are you a romantic at heart?"

No, I want to say. Not if the past six months have taught me anything. But I think better about answering, which would draw Evan's attention to me and piss Sammie off even more. "I don't really have an opinion on the subject—" I start to say.

"Of course you don't!" Professor Cox interrupts me with a laugh. "That's because you haven't lived yet. Not really.

None of you. You don't know about love or loss or grief or sadness. You think you do because you've been through a few hardships here and there, but you don't."

Evan comes to my defense. "Now that's not fair, Professor Cox. We don't know the first thing about Viviana here—"

"None of you," Professor Cox repeats. He isn't laughing anymore. His face has turned sour and grim. "You don't know what it means to suffer."

Excuse me?

I don't know about sadness? Sammie doesn't know about grief?

I'm overcome with the desire to scream. Or slap him. This stranger. This man who doesn't know the first thing about me. How dare he comment on my life. On any of our lives.

"You don't know anything about us," I say.

"I know *everything* about you," Professor Cox says, his twitching eyes hollow and cold. "I know why you're all hopeless romantics who think that there's going to be a happily ever after every single time."

"See, you don't know me one bit," I snap back. "Who said I ever believed in happily ever after?"

"Wait," Evan says. "You don't believe in love?" He's sort of unreasonably outraged at my question, or my declaration, or whatever it is that I'm trying to fight against.

I don't know how to respond.

I stand up. And when I do, I feel it. It all floods back. The fluttering. The dizziness. The pounding drum of my chest. My lungs empty and shallow.

I only just got here, I've only just sat down, but I want to leave. If I could, I would walk right out of here, back upstairs, down the street, anywhere. But I don't want to lose this job, so I walk toward the pool. There's one old lady doing laps in the deep end and a few preschoolers bouncing in the shallow end with their moms. Vanessa's on duty. She asks if I'm okay, and I tell her that I just need a minute, and she says okay, and then she lets me sit at the bottom of her ladder without asking me any more questions.

It's starting to rush back through me, Sammie's dad, my mom's cancer, my dad leaving, Dean, the bike incident. All of it.

I stick my feet in the water. It's cold. It calms me down, but it's not enough. My heart's still racing; my breath is caught.

I don't have a bathing suit on, just my leggings and a tank top that I wore to school, but I jump in anyway. I plunge myself under the water. It fills my eyes and fills my ears. I swim away from Vanessa's chair to the other side of the pool, where I hold on to the quiet corner ledge.

I am gasping for breath. I float on my back and force myself to take a deep gulp of air, and it fills me, calms me, lets me settle.

I can breathe.

I am calm.

I beat it this time.

I dive back underwater and swim in wide circles around the empty pool. I let everything above the surface turn blurry and distant. I force it all to fade away. I force it all to disappear.

College Admissions Tip #5

Even more than good grades and constant activity, college admissions boards want to see that you demonstrate integrity in your commitments. There's merit in exhibiting loyalty in whatever it is you choose to do.

I am completely submerged in the deep end of the pool when I hear a faint splash from the shallow end. I swim to the surface, expecting to see Vanessa coming to see if I'm okay, but to my surprise, it's Evan, and he's swimming my way. I look out toward the office—Sammie's gone, as is Professor Cox. Great. Now she'll really hate me. My attempt to deflect attention from my Episode has not just failed; it's accomplished the exact opposite of what I intended.

Evan approaches, with a soft, concerned smile on his face. "You okay?"

I nod, but I don't want to say anything to complicate this situation any more. The less I say, the better. That being said, I can't help but smile a little at the fact that Evan's also fully clothed in his sweatshirt and sweatpants, that he jumped straight in after me and is now completely drenched.

He treads water next to me. "So, is this, like, the opposite of skinny-dipping?"

"Something like that." I force the words out through heavy breaths. "I guess." I am considerably calmer but still know that I'm at the edge of an Episode, and the mix of swimming and talking is making it worse. I motion that I want to swim over to the closest ladder.

We each grab a rung and hold on, the water bobbing and lapping around us. There's a weird kind of quiet here in this corner of the pool, even now that he's next to me. I know I should get out of the water, dry off, find Sammie, apologize—again—for being so careless. But I also feel like I should stay to offer some explanation to Evan, or to say thank you, or to tell him something—anything—since he offered this grand gesture of drenching himself for me.

"You didn't have to jump in after me," I say finally. "I'm not drowning or anything."

Evan smiles and wipes the dripping water from his eyes. "I know you're not drowning."

"Then why are you here?"

Evan bites his lip and then says, "You can't let Professor Cox get to you. You can't take him seriously."

I shake my head. "It's not just Professor Cox. It's a lot more than Professor Cox."

"I'm a good listener," he says with a smile. Even though we're both fully clothed, there's something strangely intimate about being this close to him, the only two people in the pool. I realize that the last time I was alone with him was at Anne Boyd's party. I wonder if he remembers. It hits me that the other reason I'm having trouble leaving is because of how nice it is to be here together, sort of hiding from everyone under the edge of the pool.

"You don't want to talk?"

I do, I think. *Desperately*. And I feel like Evan's someone who could listen, who could ask the right questions, who maybe even understands.

He moves closer to me. "I'd really like to get to know you better." He places his hand on my forearm, and my promise to Sammie floods back, along with the dizziness and nausea.

I pull my arm back, shake my head, and try for something cold instead: "I don't need you to save me. Thanks, though." I start to climb up the ladder. My clothes, heavy with water, feel like they're trying to pull me back into the pool.

"Oh God. I'm sorry. I never said I was here to save you."

I turn around. "Isn't this part of your job? Saving flailing victims from drowning? Do I look like I'm that pathetic?"

He doesn't answer at first. Instead, he just sort of stares at me, stunned, like I'm not making any sense. Probably because I'm not.

"Seriously, Viviana. I just wanted to see if you're okay,"

he says, finally. He climbs up to the top rung. "Look. I just have to say it. I like you. I do. And I'm here for you, if you need anything. Is that the worst thing in the world?"

Yes, I think. *For so many reasons, it really, really is.*

But I don't say this. I don't say anything. Instead, I leave him there in the water and head out of the pool and back upstairs, the complete, dripping mess that I am.

Thankfully, Sammie doesn't hate me. In fact, she's the one who texts me first. She writes that (1) she's sorry she walked out on me, (2) she wants to know if I'm okay, and (3) can we meet up on the roof after dinner. I write back *(1) It's okay, (2) I'm okay, and (3) Yes, please, ASAP.* I decide that instead of trying to apologize via text, I'll tell her what happened with Evan in the water, and I'll say I'm sorry in person. It's time to lay it all out on the table, be completely honest with her.

When I get upstairs, Sammie has two mugs of hot coffee and a brand-new package of Oreos ready for us. It's dark, but the entire city is lit up and alive. It's the perfect time to tell her everything—and I do want to—but I'm not sure exactly how to start or what to say. Where do I even start? *Sorry, it sucks, but he likes me, not you?* How do you even say that to your friend? What words do you use to break your friend's heart, even if it is just a crush?

So we sit mostly in silence on the plastic lounge chairs and spend the night working our way through half the cookies. We spy on apartments across the street and braid each other's hair, and I'm grateful for the fact that she's not asking me about what happened yet. She gives me a crown braid, so that my hair wraps over my head, which I can never do myself, and I braid hers into a half waterfall. Sammie plays with a new app that lets her take artistic night photos and then has me take some shots of her hair for her Instagram. She hovers over her phone while I lie on my back and look up at the sky. I count four stars, two airplanes, and one helicopter, and then I close my eyes and listen to the buzz of the city below us. I love being up here with her. We're twenty-eight stories into the sky, away from everyone and everything, but perfectly good together.

"My hair looks so good," she says. "This will get a lot of likes. Thanks."

"You're welcome." I open my eyes and look over at her.

Sammie finally puts down her phone and breaks the silence: "Okay, what was that?"

I sit up. "I don't know."

"But, like, what happened? Why did you walk off like that?"

I shrug. "I guess I was just offended. I mean, what an ass. How dare he say we don't know about life."

"I get that. But what's with the dramatic exit? That kind of performance is my specialty." She laughs quietly. "You know that."

I have to tell her. "Evan jumped in after me. After you left."

"What do you mean he 'jumped in'?"

"He got into the water with all of his clothes on." I force a laugh to make it sound like it was something silly, something light. "He was playing lifeguard or something, I think."

"But Vanessa was on duty," she says. "Ugh. This is ridiculous. He likes you, not me." She can see straight though me.

I try a different route. "Well, even if he does, I'm pretty sure that I've sufficiently convinced Evan that I'm certifiable, so I don't think he'll be expressing any further interest in me. Now he's really all yours."

I hope this works. Even though he may be into me, which I've just admitted, I'm absolutely determined not to go for him. I'm absolutely determined not to go for anyone. If Sammie knew that I even remotely like him, she'd back off, which would be pointless. As far as I'm concerned, he's fair game.

Sammie gives me a half-skeptical, half-hopeful look. "So you're saying you think I should go for him? That it's okay if I go for him."

"Of course," I say. And I'm being honest. It really is okay.

"I mean, he wasn't as much of a jerk today," she says. "All that talk about true love and his dreams and that stuff with his dad. He seems really sweet, actually."

"That's true."

She picks up her phone and opens his Instagram page. "Look how cute he is, with his guitar."

She clicks on it and plays a clip of him strumming a Bon Iver song. "He'd make a good boyfriend, don't you think?"

"I wouldn't know what a good boyfriend is."

She doesn't respond to my pathetic burst of self-pity. Instead, she just sighs and puts away her phone. We lie under the clear, dark sky a little longer, and thankfully the conversation shifts to finals and senior year and then to less important stuff, like the pros and cons of fried Oreos and our lack of plans for my upcoming birthday, which is on the Fourth of July.

At midnight, we head back downstairs and climb into her bed, where Sammie continues to play on Instagram while I lie awake, trying not to think about my most recent Episode and why I reacted the way I did. Or Evan. Or how much Sammie likes him. Or how cute he was in that clip.

Sammie's off today on a mysterious errand with her mom, one that she won't tell me about. I assume it has something do with my birthday in a few weeks. Even though I told her she doesn't have to do or get anything for me, she always plans some extravagant surprise, like baking me two dozen cookies from scratch or setting up a citywide scavenger hunt. She goes so far that when her birthday finally comes in August, I feel lame for not knowing how to match hers.

Since she's gone, and it's slow today, I'm actually able to get some studying done. Hardly anyone has come, since it rained all morning, just a few of the hard-core lap swimmers. Virgo thought he was going to have to close the pool, but there hasn't been any lightning, just a sprinkle here and there, and there's still another hour and a half until closing. Still, poor Evan's under an umbrella on deck, waiting for an eighty-something-year-old woman to finish her water aerobics.

Virgo sits down next to me and opens the schedule binder. *"Ciao, bella.* Mind if I join you?"

"Not at all."

He looks at my book. "Aren't you done yet?"

"Nope. Three more finals."

"I do not miss high school."

"Don't you still have to take finals?"

"Sure, but a college semester's only sixteen weeks, so we were done almost a month ago. Plus, you don't have to be at school seven hours a day. You actually have time to study."

"Sounds glorious."

"I mean, it's a lot of work, but you're going to be amazed at how much easier it is than high school in a lot of ways. Especially since you're a nerd."

"Hey, I'm not a nerd!"

He flips to the back cover of my book. "You're studying for a health final. No one studies for health finals. So, yeah, you're a nerd."

"I don't want to mess up my GPA."

Virgo laughs. "You're a nerd. But believe me, that's a good thing. You'll rule the world one day."

I thank him because I know he's saying it to be nice, not to mock me, but I can't help but feel a little self-conscious.

A few minutes later, Evan approaches the desk. "Last person just got out, finally," he says. Then he jumps on the counter and sits so his legs are right next to my book. He tries to catch my eye, to offer me a smile that reads like maybe a request or an apology, or, at the very least, a plea for a truce.

I slide a few inches away, close my book, and slide it under the counter.

"God, I hope no one else shows up," Virgo says.

"Can we close this place yet?" Evan complains. "I mean, look how dark the sky is."

"Sorry," Virgo says. "Only if you see lightning, or if a kid hurls in the pool."

Evan looks at me. "Don't you have a little sister? Any fake vomit upstairs you can bring down?"

I laugh. "Somewhere in her disaster of a room, I'm sure."

Right then, the sky lights up with a flash and then a few seconds later everything vibrates with the booming echo of thunder.

Evan claps his hands and jumps off the counter. "There's your lightning! Bennett Tower Pool is officially closed!"

Virgo heads off to tell the eighty-something-year-old woman that she has to get out of the water, and then he goes to lock up all the bathrooms. Evan and I work on putting away a few chairs and cleaning up the office.

I shut down the computers and close up the sign-in binders while Evan organizes the pH test kits. Even with the pounding rain and Virgo's operatic voice reverberating down the hall, there's an awkward silence between us. It's the heavy weight of an unfinished conversation, one that I don't want to have. I can tell he wants to talk to me because he keeps looking over at me, trying to catch my eye. Part of me wants to talk to him, too, to explain what happened the other day and why I can't get involved with anyone right now and maybe even drop hints about how Sammie likes him. But I decide that the best thing to do right now is focus on cleaning up—that is, on keeping my mouth shut and eyes forward.

He locks up the last cabinet and then breaks the silence.

"So we have this surprise gift of an hour or so. We should hang out or something."

"Um, no. I need to study. Three finals this week. But thanks."

Virgo comes into the office, drenched and smiling. "I love rain."

"Let's do something, yeah?" Evan says. "Viviana is going to call up Sammie and tell her to come hang out with us."

"I never said I was going to—"

"Come on," Evan says. "You need a break. See if Sammie's home yet. Tell her to come."

Now I'm totally confused. Why is he telling me to call Sammie? Is this part of his appeal for a truce? I really want to say no, but Sammie would kill me if I passed up this opportunity for a health final.

Evan looks at me. "We could all just hang out. Tell her to come."

"Okay, yeah, I guess. Hold on." I text her: *URGENT. Lover boy wants to know if you're home yet. Pool is closed due to lightning storm and he wants to hang out. Where are you?*

I get an immediate text in return: *HELL YASSS. Stuck in traffic but will be there sooooooon. Say yes and I will join you.*

"Sammie's in."

"Excellent," Evan says. "Virgo, you in?"

"Sure." He shrugs. "I've got nothing to do."

Evan looks at me. "Could we go up to your place?"

"No, my mom's studying and my sister's there, probably finding ten million ways to distract her. We could go to the roof of my building. There's an indoor room. It's used for parties, but when it's not rented out, it's open to anyone.

And it's actually great during a storm. When it thunders, the whole building rattles. But it's even better up there. Mila says it's like being inside a drum."

"That sounds like absolute perfection," Evan says.

Virgo agrees, and we run through the rain to the back door of Bennett Tower. I pull out my key and make a silent prayer to the gods of precipitation and other random occurrences that I don't run into my mom or Mila in the elevator.

Thankfully, the gods are in good spirits today. We arrive at the top floor, to find the windows of the party room encased in thick gray clouds.

The room is empty except for some folded chairs and a Ping-Pong table. "Fantastic," Evan says. "I haven't played in years." He finds a couple of paddles and balls under the table and motions to Virgo and me. "Two against one?"

I take a paddle. "I have to warn you. I've spent many hours up here. I'm a bit of a pro."

"A pro, huh?" Evan picks up a ball and dribbles it on the table. "That sounds like a challenge. I'm in."

Virgo takes his paddle and stands next to me. "I'm on her team."

I text Sammie to let her know where we are, and then I take my position.

As it turns out, I am better than both Evan and Virgo, but generally speaking, we all kind of suck.

Evan is about to serve the ball to us when he stops. "Time out. Have you ever played Extreme Ping-Pong?"

"No." Virgo and I both laugh.

"I am not familiar with Extreme Ping-Pong," I say.

"Well, it's a game where only the chosen few, only the

truly daring, triumph," Evan says. "The goal is to keep the ball off the floor, by any means possible. Other than that, there are no rules. Only survival. Do you think you two are brave enough to survive?"

What begins as a serious game with points and careful serves and rules about volleying and double bounces quickly devolves into a ridiculous game of full-room tennis. We're leaping and diving and running around the room, hitting the ball so that it flies off the walls, off the ceilings, off our paddles two, three, four times, anything to keep the ball from the ground. And we're on a streak. It has to be a good five solid minutes of the ball moving through the air before a flash of lightning fills up the room and thunder reverberates so loudly that Evan, who's in control of the ball, drops it and shudders from the bang.

"Dude," Virgo yells. "You killed our streak!"

"Holy crap!" Evan fumbles for the ball. "You weren't kidding. That is terrifying!"

"I told you!" I laugh.

Virgo slams his paddle on the table and high-fives me. "And that means Viviana and I are the triumphant World Champions of Extreme Ping-Pong!"

"The tournament isn't over yet," Evan says. "It's only just begun."

Virgo checks his phone. "Sorry, man. I've got to get out of here. Meeting my girl for dinner."

I check my phone. Sammie hasn't texted back yet. I text her again: *You on your way? Not sure how much longer we'll all be here. Virgo's leaving. Come quick. I'm saving lover boy 4 u.*

Virgo leaves, and it's just Evan and me and the thunder

and lightning. There are patches of blue now in the sky, but the rain's still pounding down pretty hard. "Want to just watch the storm?" he asks.

"Sure," I say. We put the paddles back and sit on the floor at the edge of the window. This very large party room suddenly feels very small now that Virgo's gone.

Outside the window, the sky is thick with clouds. On clear days, we can see all of the city from up here—Lake Michigan, the Hancock Building and all of Michigan Avenue to the east, Willis Tower and all of downtown to the south. Now, the entire city's disappeared behind the storm, and it's just us: Evan and me, and no one else. I suddenly feel like I'm sitting too close to him. I slide a few inches away, and I make it look like it's so I can rest my back against the wall.

"You okay?"

"What?" I say. "Yeah, I'm fine."

"That was a fun game."

"It was." I look at my phone. No text from Sammie. "I don't know why she isn't writing back."

"Who?"

"Sammie," I say.

"Right." There's more lightning. Evan presses his head against the window and counts under his breath, and then the thunder rumbles, enough to shake the whole building again. "Ten miles away. Looks like it's moving this way."

I check my phone again: 6:35. Nothing. "I should probably get going soon."

Evan lifts his head and looks at me. "I'm sorry Professor Cox upset you. He can be brutal sometimes."

"Brutal," I say with a laugh. "Okay, if that's what you want to call it."

"He's a good man, really. And he speaks some very real truths that, as much as they're difficult to hear, can be incredibly enlightening."

"I just—you know what? Never mind."

"What?"

"Well—I don't understand, why you like him so much, I mean. He doesn't seem that smart to me—brutal, sure—but I don't see that there's much to like about him."

Evan turns around, presses his back against the window, and thinks for a minute. "I think he's had a really hard life. He's told me a few things and—" I'm about to ask him what things, when Evan looks at me. "Professor Cox was the only one who knows that I've changed my major to music. Well, now him—and you."

"Oh."

"He's the first person who told me that I should do what I want with my life. That it's my life to live. That I'm not allowed to live according to my father's logic. My dad's dream is for me to be a CEO of some corporation. He only signed me up for violin because playing an instrument is supposed to help you be better at math. I could hardly even hold a pencil, and yet he had me holding a violin and a bow and going to classes two times a week and making me wake up every day before school to practice at five A.M. Only it completely backfired on him, because I'm mediocre at math, but apparently I'm a whiz at music."

I nod. "My dad makes me untangle all my knots."

"What?"

"He has all these rules. One is called 'Learning from past mistakes.' Like, he absolutely hates when my cords get all tangled. Headphones. Computer cords." I laugh. "And a necklace? God forbid. He says, 'If you'd just take a minute to do it right, you'll save yourself hours of frustration later. Learn from your past mistakes, Viviana. Learn, and change your future behaviors.' But the thing is, he's the one who's frustrated by it. They're my cords, my necklaces, so why do they bother him?"

"Here," he says, reaching for the strings on my hoodie.

I laugh. "What are you doing?"

He leans in close and ties the end of each string into a double and then a triple knot. His fingers brush the skin on my neck, and I can't help but shiver.

"There," Evan says. "Your knots are none of his business."

His eyes meet mine, and we both smile. Lightning streaks across the sky and we start counting in unison—"One one thousand, two one thousand, three one thousand"—all the way to five one thousand, when the building shakes around us with what feels like an explosion of thunder. Even though we knew it was coming, we both jump. He grabs for my hands at the same time that I grab for his, and we're suddenly holding each other tight, and then we're laughing at the ridiculousness of our own surprise.

His hands are warm around mine, and I don't want to let go.

Stop it, Viviana, I think. *Learn from your past mistakes.*

I pull my hands out of his grip and scoot a few inches away.

"So, my dad has rules, too," Evan says. I'm thankful that

he's the first to break the silence. "First one: No crying. My dad likes to say 'CEOs don't cry, son.' Like he would know what a CEO does or doesn't do. He's low-level management at H&R Block."

"You cry?" I ask.

"Not anymore. I used to. At sad movies and things like that. And certain songs."

"Like what?"

"'Eleanor Rigby,'" he says with a smile. "Every time." He sings a few lines for me. He has a beautiful voice. I really wish he didn't have such a beautiful voice.

"They have crying salons in Japan now," I say. "Like you can pay to sit in a room that's not your house so you can watch sad movies and cry." I feel like I'm just saying words, trying to distract us from whatever it is that's happening.

"I might actually love that. Except that they could just play Beatles songs and I'd be fine."

"But you wouldn't be allowed," I say. "It's women only."

"Sexist bastards."

"Yup." I laugh.

Evan looks at me. "I'm sorry your dad is such a jerk."

"Me, too. About yours, I mean."

"I just know that when I'm a dad, I'm going to be completely different. My kids will get to follow their hearts, no strings attached."

I smile. "That's awesome."

The sky fills up with lightning, and then, without pause, the close roaring of thunder, as though to punctuate this thought. The rumbling storm surrounds us, and I feel like we're both trying not to reach out to each other. At least, I know I'm trying.

"Why were you such a jerk to Sammie?" I ask, partly to bring his attention back to Sammie, partly because I'm curious.

"What are you talking about?"

"The whole horoscope thing. It wasn't very nice. Why were you antagonizing her like that?"

He looks shocked—and hurt. "Was I? Oh. I'm sorry. I didn't mean to be a jerk."

"Then why were you? What was that about?"

He smiles. "I guess I was trying to antagonize you."

"Why would you try to do that?"

"I already told you. I like you. I liked the fact that you were finally talking to me. I was trying to get your attention."

Great. I was trying bring thoughts of Sammie back into the room, and we end up here again.

Evan turns around and starts tracing circles on the foggy windows. He doesn't say anything else for a good minute, and I'm not sure how to respond, where to even begin.

Finally, he looks at me. "You don't remember me, do you?"

My heart leaps into my throat. "What do you mean?"

"Anne Boyd's birthday party." He bites his lip. "I think I was a freshman? You were in middle school, right?"

I don't know what to say. What to admit. What would I say if Sammie were here? Where *is* she?

I stumble to check my phone.

It's 6:55.

Nothing from Sammie.

"Do you remember me?"

I look up at him, totally and completely stumped for words.

"It took me a few days to place where I knew you from. But then, when I did, it all came back to me." He smiles. "That was a really good kiss."

My phone lights up.

"Viviana, didn't you hear me?"

I look up. "What? Sorry. Text from Sammie." I stand up and throw my phone in my bag. "Turns out she's not going to make it. The storm has flooded the roads and they're stuck on Western Avenue or something."

Evan looks confused, but he doesn't say it again; he doesn't ask again. Instead, he gets up, too.

"And I didn't realize how late it is. I've really got to get downstairs, or my mom's going to kill me." I look out the window. The storm is rolling away, but the sky is turning dark with the setting sun.

"Okay. Sure. Yeah." Evan grabs his backpack and throws it over his shoulder.

After all that sharing and avoidance, the silence in the elevator isn't just awkward; it's painful.

I get off at my floor and say a quick good-bye.

Thankfully, Evan doesn't say anything else. The doors close, and it's over.

For now.

College Admissions Tip #6

Applying to college can be stressful! While going through the process, be sure to find a creative outlet, some kind of distraction, that will help you deal with the worries about your future.

I decide not to say anything to Sammie about what happened on the roof. After giving it some thought, I figure that because I didn't respond to him, Evan got the message loud and clear that I'm not into him.

Or rather, the lie that I'm not into him.

Every time I think about our conversation, how nice it was to talk to him about my parents, to hear about his dad, to talk to someone who understands how hard it can be, I'm shaken. And then I think about what he said to me, about how pretty he thinks I am, about that stupidly amazing fifteen-second kiss that happened more than four years ago, and I know it's a lie.

I'm lying to Sammie and I'm lying to myself.

I'm totally into him.

But denying it is my only choice. I mean, it's the kind thing, right? I refuse to be the one to break Sammie's heart. And there's no point in getting in her way.

My mind is distracted by this new, stupid complication, and I have to do everything to breathe my way through the week, not to let any more Episodes happen. I get through finals, somehow. Grades won't be posted until next week, but I get a real day off today, the kind that my mom has wanted for me since that day I fell off my bike. I do have to hang out with Mila, though. It's Sunday, but my mom has a meeting with her lawyer about the separation stuff. Since I don't have to work, Sammie and I decide to take Mila down to the pool. Except for my one panic-driven immersion, I haven't really been in the water yet, not for, like, a relaxing, fun summer swim.

We arrive at noon, and the pool is swarming with families and their kids.

"It's crazy busy again," I say. "Don't tell me it's going to be like this the rest of the summer."

"Not really," Sammie says. "We'll try to get mostly week-day shifts, when the kids are all at camp."

We leave our stuff in the office locker and head to the water. Sammie's wearing her very small bikini—so small, in fact, that even Mila is pointing and mouthing at me: *I can see her butt.* I ignore her.

Before we get in, Sammie asks me to take some photos of her for Instagram. She has me do this by the deep end, so that she's in direct view of Evan, who's on duty on the lifeguard chair.

"I want to look like this." Before she hands me her phone, she flashes it in my face to show me a black-and-white photo of Marilyn Monroe sitting on the edge of an empty pool; her feet dangle in the water, and her arms stretch behind her, so that her breasts are perky and high.

"Well, don't we all?"

"I mean, I'm going to sit like this, and I'm not going to look at the camera. I'm going to look up above your head, so that it looks like I'm flirting with someone, like she is. Just see if you can get the angle right."

"Okay." I take the phone from her and switch it to the camera mode. "I'll try." Sammie takes her pose, legs stretched, back arched, chin angled up. I crouch down and take a few shots. Mila's leaning against my back, looking over my shoulder—right at Evan, of course—as I take the pics. He's wearing mirrored sunglasses, though, so it's hard to tell if he's actually even looking at her.

"You look pretty, Sammie," Mila says.

Sammie does look pretty—I mean she always looks pretty—and I know that whatever photo I take of her will be beautiful. A few kids, maybe middle schoolers, decide to have a cannonball contest right next to our photo shoot. It's completely on purpose, and I can't help but laugh. They're about to jump in, when Sammie yells at them. "Hey, can you move your contest to the other side of the deck?"

They giggle at her mischievously, but they don't argue.

Once they're gone, I take a few more shots and then show her. "There are a bunch of kids in the background."

She looks at the phone and then hands it back to me. "I don't care about that. But can you, like, angle it so my double chin isn't showing?"

I try not to groan, but I can't help it. First of all, she doesn't have a double chin. And I wish she wouldn't say that stuff around Mila. The kid is completely confident and sure of herself, and I want her to stay that way. "It's hot out here, Sammie," I grumble. "I just want to go in the water."

"Just a few more shots. Please?"

"Can I try?" Mila asks. "I have a really good eye for pictures. I watch TV, like, all day."

"It's sad but true," I say. "Both that she watches TV all day and that she's a much better photographer than me." When I was Mila's age, my parents were on me to spend all my extra time reading, but Mila gets to do whatever she wants in a way I never did.

"Sure," Sammie says. "Go for it."

I hand Mila the phone, and she gets this very adult look on her face. She's focused and determined, full of intent. She chooses one angle, then shakes her head and tries another one. She takes about ten photos.

"Employing children now?" Evan yells from his perch. "Aren't there laws against that?"

My stomach goes hollow with the sight of him, but thankfully he doesn't look at me.

"Very funny," Sammie says, and she flips her hair.

Mila hands Sammie her phone. "These should be good," she says.

Sammie scrolls through the photos and laughs. "These are perfect, Mila. Thank you! I'm going to hire you as my official photographer."

Mila's beaming with the compliment.

"Can we go in now?" I ask.

"Yes, you can go in now," Sammie says before she heads back to the office to put her phone away.

Mila and I jump in, finally. It feels perfect. Cold. Fresh. Mila swims over to me and wraps her arms around my shoulders. "Give me a ride!" she yells.

I laugh and pretend to be a magical dolphin for her. She even makes me squeal.

This is exactly what I needed. To be laughing. To be submerged and silly and separated from the incessant reminders of the past six months, how everything's changed. I'm here with Mila, and she hasn't changed. Not yet. She still loves me as much as she did before I messed everything up.

I'm having so much fun, I'm able to wipe it all from my mind.

Mila jumps off my back and splashes me in the face. I splash her back.

"Hey, you guys, watch out!" Sammie has returned and is now planted on the edge of the pool again, this time closer to the lifeguard chair. There's no camera, but she's still mimicking Marilyn Monroe.

"Aren't you coming in?" Mila asks.

"Maybe," she says, and then she slides her hair over her shoulder. "In a little bit."

She's posing for Evan, trying to get his eyes back on her. I turn to Mila. "Race?"

She nods and dashes out toward the shallow end. I leave Sammie to play her flirting game with Evan. I follow Mila, pretending to swim at full power, even though, of course, I'm going to let her win.

We get to the rope of the shallow end, and Mila announces her victory.

I laugh and hug her tight.

And then I can't help it. I glance up at the chair. The pool is packed with kids—with school out, summer is finally in full swing—and Evan's not paying attention to Sammie. Not at all.

He's in work mode, scanning the pool back and forth to make sure everyone's safe.

He stops and lifts his sunglasses. He looks straight at me. And he smiles.

I dive under the water and stay there as long as I can so that Sammie doesn't see, before Mila pulls me up, only to splash water right in my face.

Tic-tac-toe.
Hit me high.
Hit me low.
Hit me three in a row.
Gonna get hit by a UFO!
Gonna get hit by a UFO!
Gonna get hit by a UFO!

Rock, paper, scissors.
I win, you lose.
Now you get a big bruise.
You win, fair and square.
Now I get to pull your hair.

"Wait, so whoever loses has to get punched, and whoever wins has to get their hair pulled? Where did you learn this awful game, Mila?" We just got out of the water after a good three hours, and we're sitting on some lounge chairs near the office. Mila's teaching Sammie and me these clapping games that are much darker than I ever remember.

"What happened to Miss Suzie and her steamboat?"

Sammie laughs. "That one was pretty dark, if I remember correctly. 'Her steamboat went to hell, ding, ding'?"

"Oh yeah," I say. "And then didn't Miss Suzie sit upon a piece of glass—"

Sammie continues: "And broke her little ass—"

"Ask me no more questions—"

"I'll tell you no more lies."

"The boys are in the bathroom, and they're pulling up their flies—" We sing this in unison.

"Ew!" Mila screams. "That's disgusting! At least mine's not disgusting!"

"But yours is mean, Mila," I say. "You and your friends hit each other?"

Mila nods. "On the back."

"Hard?"

Mila nods again.

Sammie laughs. "Do it to me."

"Okay." Mila shrugs. "Turn around." Sammie does, and then Mila whacks her smack in the middle of her back. Hard. Really hard.

"Ow!" Sammie yelps. "That really hurt!"

"Mila! Say you're sorry!"

"I'm sorry," Mila says. "But that's how hard my friends and I do it to each other." She's not even remotely upset by the fact that I am. In fact, she's proud of the abuse that she and her friends inflict upon one another.

"Now you get to pull my hair," Mila says to Sammie, laughing.

"I'm not going to pull your hair," Sammie says. "Friends aren't supposed to hurt each other."

Friends aren't supposed to hurt each other.

"Okay, fine. I'll pull my own hair," Mila says, and then she does, really hard, and then she laughs. "That hurt."

"You're crazy, little girl," Sammie says.

Evan comes over and sits on the chair next to Mila, right across from me. "What in God's name are you doing to yourself?"

"It's a game. Want to play? I promise I won't pull your hair."

"Are you going to hit me like you hit Sammie?"

"Maybe." Mila laughs.

"No, thank you." He looks at me. "Is she always this abusive?"

"She's always this wild," I say.

"Am not," Mila says, scrunching up her face at me. "Can

we go to the zoo now? I want to see the baby gorilla that was born last week."

"Seriously? You want to go to the zoo now? Aren't you exhausted?"

"I'm surprised you're not totally passed out," Sammie says. "You guys were in the water for, what, three hours?"

"Yeah." Mila holds up her hands. "My fingers are like dried cranberries."

"Dried cranberries?" Evan says. "How gourmet! Mine only turn into raisins."

"Can we go back in the water?" Mila whines. "I want to swim more."

"I need a break," I say.

"What about you, Sammie?" Mila begs. "Come in with me?"

Sammie, who spent the entire three hours sunbathing on the side of the pool, shakes her head no.

"Why didn't you get in, Sammie?" Mila asks.

"Yeah," Evan says. "Why didn't you get in, Sammie?" He's teasing her, and though I'm sure she likes the attention, I can tell she's embarrassed to give the real reason: She's dressed for Evan, and if she were to swim, her hair and makeup would get messed up.

She shrugs. "Just didn't feel like it."

"So no one's going to go back in with me?"

"Well, I just clocked out and was about to do my laps," Evan says. "I can skip a few and swim with you. Want to play Marco Polo?"

"Yes!" Mila perks up.

Evan looks at me. "Is that okay?"

"Sure."

And then he starts staring at me, at my eyes—like he won't look away. "What?" I ask.

"You have extremely large pupils," he says.

"Um, okay . . . ," I mumble, not knowing what else to say to such a bizarre statement.

"I mean, I don't mean to stare, but scientifically speaking, it means that you are an attractive person."

"What?" I can feel the blood rush to my cheeks from embarrassment.

"Men are attracted to large pupils," he says. "It's been studied. I learned about it in psych this year. From Professor Cox, of course. Women in Italy used to use a plant called belladonna to dilate their pupils to attract men. You wouldn't even need it. You have this natural ability to do so."

"To attract men?" I spurt out with a laugh.

"Yes," he says, smiling. "To attract men."

At first, I smile back at him, but then it hits me that this is a weird, private thing he's saying and we have a weird, public audience of both my little sister, who's grinning romantically at us, and Sammie, who's giving me a sharp look of death.

Great.

Mila breaks the awkward silence between us by pulling on Evan's arm. "Are we going in or what?"

That breaks Evan's stare. He claps his hands and jumps up. "Let's do it!"

Mila throws off her towel and starts to run to the pool

until Evan calls out his "No running" warning in his official lifeguard tone, and she slows to a run-walk.

This leaves Sammie and me alone, and me worried about what she's going to say.

"Look, Sammie, I'm sorry. I have no idea what that was about."

But Sammie's not angry anymore. Instead, her shoulders are slumped, her head in her hands. "Forget it, Vivi," she says. "It's done. I'm over it. He's into you. No bikini is going to change that."

"We don't know that for sure."

She looks up at me. "Um, your pupils are so large that they attract men? I think we *do* know for sure." She stands up and wraps a towel around her waist. "No hard feelings or anything, but I've got to go."

"Come on, Sammie—"

"You don't have to run after me. And I'm not mad. I just need to be alone, okay?"

"Okay," I say. "Hang out tonight maybe?"

"Maybe," she says, and then she grabs her bag from the office locker and leaves.

Evan and Mila are in the pool, racing from one end to the other. He's letting her win, and she's howling with delight. I want to rush after Sammie, but I promised I wouldn't. I hate this. I hate it that she likes him and that he maybe, probably likes me and that I don't have any idea what I feel about him. Let me rephrase. What I hate the most is that I probably do like him, but I don't want to admit it. I don't want to hurt Sammie, but even more, I don't want to trust anyone else. I don't want to feel attraction or liking or anything that could possibly lead to love.

And I hate that. I hate the fact that I can't let myself feel.

And then what I do feel is that rush of dizziness wash over me, and my heart starts to pound in my throat. It's the anxiety, the panic, flooding over me. I know this. This, at least, is familiar. I lean back in my chair and close my eyes. I close my eyes and try to breathe.

I lie like this for a while, trying to just focus on breathing in and breathing out. The sounds of the pool are around me—most of the families are gone already, but there are a few kids running and splashing, the chatter of their parents, and Mila's laughter, distant but most familiar.

I actually breathe and calm myself down enough that I start to fall asleep. I let the exhaustion wash over me. I let my body relax. I let myself drift. And I'm on that far edge of sleep when I'm startled awake by screaming— Mila's screams, Evan's screams, the guards, the families, all screaming around me.

I open my eyes and find that everyone is not only screaming; they're running, too, out of the pool, toward the umbrellas. They're running and ducking and pointing at the sky.

"Run, Viviana!" Mila's screaming at me from an umbrella near the edge of the pool.

I look up and see what look like bright orange-red grenades falling from the sky.

"It's the Nut!" Mila yells. "He's throwing tomatoes!"

"Come here!" Evan screams at me. "Before you get hit! Fast! Run!"

I don't have time to think. I should run toward the office, which is much closer than where Evan and Mila are, but my instinct is to be with my sister, especially since we're under attack, and so I run toward them. Thankfully, I move just in time before a tomato falls, splat, on my towel, where I had been sitting mere seconds before.

"What the hell!" I laugh as I squeeze under their umbrella, where they've been joined by at least two other families and their kids, who are all soaking wet. "He's lost his mind completely!"

One of the dads yells up at Professor Cox. "Stop throwing those! You'll kill someone!"

He's right, but I can't help but laugh at the absurdity of the tomato grenades being launched from the eleventh floor. A tomato lands right on our umbrella, which makes me laugh even harder.

Professor Cox's throwing dozens of tomatoes. I'm not sure if he's aiming at us or at the water, but most of them splatter on concrete, and a few actually make it into the pool. We're close enough that I can see the pulpy masses turn to slime and spiral through water. Crimson fireworks explode against the pale blue floor of the pool.

Virgo, who's standing at the edge of the office, starts to sing a deep operatic aria in Italian; his baritone voice reverberates throughout the pool area. It's the most perfect sound track to this utterly ridiculous event.

That makes me explode into laughter. My laughter makes Mila start to giggle, which, in turn, makes Evan laugh, too, and then we're all giggling uncontrollably as the dad yells at the sky. Then he turns to us and snaps, "You think this is funny?"

I try to muffle my laughter and shake my head no, but really, I do think it's funny. I think this is the most ridiculous thing I've ever seen.

I look over at Evan, who's wearing the broadest, most joyful smile.

In this moment, I'm not thinking about anything.

And it's amazing.

Before I know it, I'm reaching out for Evan's hand.

He's startled for a moment, but then he looks at me with a smile and squeezes mine.

I lean in.

And I kiss him.

First, I can feel his surprise, but then I feel his decision to return the kiss. I close my eyes to let myself feel this moment, my lips on his, his mouth turning from a smile into a kiss.

And then I remember where we are.

I open my eyes and pull away before Mila sees us.

Evan smiles and squeezes my hand again.

Virgo's still singing, and the tomatoes are still falling, but at a slower rate now. Professor Cox seems to have perfected his aim, as they're all falling straight into the empty pool beside us.

Five more tomatoes fall, and then it's over.

Virgo stops his singing, and then Professor Cox calls out, "Triumph is mine!" And then: "All clear on deck!"

We wait for a few minutes, just to be sure.

Evan's hand is still wrapped around mine. We're all squeezed in close enough under this umbrella that Mila can't see.

I don't want to pull away.

Finally, everyone starts to clear out from under the umbrellas, and Evan and I are forced to let go.

I dive in the water.

Mila and Evan both follow me in. Without saying anything about the tomato attack or the sudden kiss or the touch of his strong fingers around mine, we lead the cleanup of the tomato bombs from the bottom of the pool.

The strange thing is, while I'm stunned by my own choice to kiss him, I don't feel the panic that I did mere minutes before.

As I dive the eight feet underwater, searching for the drenched fruits, I am strangely calm, strangely happy. All I can think about is how fine I am in this moment. I know I should feel upset about Sammie, about this sudden strange entanglement with Evan, about the consequences of all my bad decisions.

But none of that is weighing on me at all.

All I can think about is diving down to the bottom of this pool to find these tomatoes.

I am right here swimming. I am right here laughing. And that's enough.

The last hour has been absolutely absurd and absolutely wonderful.

For the first time in a very long time, I feel fine.

I feel really, really fine.

When we get back upstairs, Mila is still hyper from the tomato attack. I open the door, and she runs to the window.

"I can't see anything from here," she whines. "Could we go up to Sammie's? She said she can see right into his apartment, right?"

"We're not bothering Sammie right now," I say.

My mom, who's sitting at the dining room table, looks up from her papers. "What are you two talking about?"

"The Nut!" Mila exclaims, her forehead still pressed against the window. "He went crazy today! Threw tomatoes at us! It was awesome!"

My mom looks at me. "Are you talking about Professor Cox?"

"Yeah." I laugh. "He stood on his balcony and threw like fifty tomatoes at us."

"Made a huge mess!" Mila turns from the window. "Do you think he'll be arrested?"

"Someone called the police?" my mom asks.

"No. Not yet. I mean, I don't think so," I say. "But one guy, some upset dad, was threatening to. I don't know if he did."

"That would be a shame," my mom says. Then she grabs her phone to text someone. I lean over close enough that I can see she's texting Sammie's mom.

"What's his story, Mama?" I say.

She pulls her phone from my view and shakes her head.

"Come on," I say. "Tell me. What's going on?"

"None of it is your business," she says, still texting. Then she puts down her phone. "Your father called today."

"Daddy called?" Mila runs from the window to the table. "Is he home? Where is he?"

My mom bites the side of her mouth and then says, "No. He is not home."

"But wait," I say. "When I talked to him, he said he'd be home by now."

"You talked to Daddy?" Mila yells at me. "I want to talk to Daddy! I haven't gotten to talk to him in like a month!"

My mom ignores Mila. "He said he *might* be home by now. Not that he definitely would."

Mila's crying now. "I want to talk to Daddy!" she repeats. "It's not fair! You guys get to talk to him, but I don't. I'm never part of anything."

"Mila. Sit down." My mom shuffles some papers out of the way. "Both of you. I need to talk to you."

I don't like this. I was just in a good mood—the best mood—and I want to stay that way, even if it's for one night. Or at least for more than ten minutes. "I don't want to."

"Viviana, come on," she says. "Sit. This is important."

Mila's looking at me through her wet, glossy eyes for a cue of what to do, so I sit down. Mila wipes her nose with her sleeve and takes the chair next to me.

"Your father won't be home for a while," my mom says. "Not until September."

Mila doesn't understand. "So Daddy won't be home for our birthdays?"

Mila and I were born 7 years and 364 days apart—her birthday is on the third of July, and mine is on the fourth. I remember being mad at my mom that she couldn't hold Mila in one more day so that I could have a baby as my birthday present.

My mom shakes her head. "He is busy with this job. And, well, when he comes back in September, he will find a new apartment and move his things then."

So that's it. It's official. It's happening.

"What are you talking about?" Mila asks. "What does that mean?"

"It means the trial separation is over," I say. "It means they're getting a divorce. It means they tried being separated and they liked it better than staying married." The words spill out, and I know they come out as mean, as maybe too direct, too honest for an eight-year-old's ears, but my mom's only going to try to mince words, to soften the blow, and I'm sick of not talking about what's really happening.

"I did not use the word *divorce*," my mom snaps at me. "Please don't say it like that. You'll upset your sister."

Mila is crying, but that's only to be expected. "That's not my fault. You can't blame me for her being upset."

"I should have talked to you separately."

"Maybe you should have," I say. I scoot over next to Mila and put my hand on her back.

"I'm sorry, Mila. I am. I just think you're right. It isn't fair that you're not part of anything, and I think you should know the truth. I think you're old enough to know the truth."

Mila shrugs my hand off her back and gives me a wild, angry glare. "I hate you both," she says. "I hate both of you so much, it hurts." And then she runs to her room and slams the door.

"Very nice," my mom says.

I don't say that I'm sorry to my mom. I mean, I am, but I'm too angry to say anything nice.

"Where is Dad now?"

"He's staying in Singapore all summer."

"So we won't even see him until then?"

"These things take time."

"Could he at least grant Mila the honor of a phone call?"

"Of course," she says. "I can talk to him about that."

"Okay, fine," I say. "Great."

"Do you have any questions for me?"

Yes. A million questions. What happened to us? When did we all fall apart? When did we stop being nice to one another? When will we be whole again? Will we ever be whole again?

"Nope," I say. "Can I be excused now?"

"I know this is difficult for you, Viviana. All of this."

"Can I be excused now?"

"Yes," my mom says. "Of course."

"Thank you," I say. I leave the room feeling 180 degrees worse than I did when I first walked in. There is no worse than this.

College Admissions Tip #7

An integral part of the college application process should be self-discovery. Colleges want to know that you're hungry for new knowledge, new experiences, new discoveries. Be a constant searcher!

I crawl under my blanket, half-expecting the waves of panic to start crashing over me. I'm ready for it: the heart palpitations, the dizziness, the nausea. I'm ready for all of it.

But it doesn't come, at first.

I'm sad, yes. I'm frustrated, yes.

But I kissed Evan. I kissed him. He kissed me.

And I see it: the stupidity of feeling better because some random guy thinks that I'm pretty and that my pupils are attractive. It shouldn't take a guy to make me feel better. It shouldn't be because of him.

And then I think about Sammie.

About how I've betrayed her.

Oh wait. Here it comes. That dizzy feeling, that tense embarrassment, that deep worry about what I've done. It's a sharp realization, one with jagged edges that stab deep. Even when I think I'm feeling good, I'm actually failing. I've failed. Again.

I text Sammie about the fight with my mom and Mila and the divorce and how my dad won't be home for another three months. I don't text her about the tomatoes or the kiss or the hand-holding underneath the umbrella situation.

She texts back for me to come upstairs.

I go back into the dining room to ask my mom if I can stay with Sammie tonight, but she's not there. I hear whispering and crying in Mila's room. I could go in, try to make amends, but I don't. I write a note for my mom—*Upstairs with Sammie*—and leave it on her keyboard.

Sammie wraps her arms around me right when I walk in. "Do you want to talk?"

This is the point where I should say yes, that I need to tell her about Evan and me. About how stupid it was of me to kiss him.

Instead, I shake my head. "Do you?"

"No," she says. "Guys are jerks. Guys of all ages. I'm sorry about your jerky dad."

I'm supposed to say "I'm sorry about your jerky Evan," but I don't.

I can't.

So I just nod. "Tell me a story?" I say.

"Of course." We head to her bedroom and lean against the window.

Sammie picks up her binoculars and tells me that the O'Briens are eating Thai. "Good for them," she says. "Shaking it up!"

"Is Professor Cox home?"

She moves her binoculars to his balcony. "No." She lifts the binoculars. "Oh, but Mrs. Woodley is belly dancing in her living room! Want to see?"

I close my eyes. "No thanks. Describe it for me?"

Sammie nods and tells me about Mrs. Woodley's new life plan to travel the world with Tad, bungee jumping in New Zealand, river kayaking in Bali, and mountain biking in Namibia.

"Mountain biking in Namibia?"

"It's a thing people do," she says. "I read about it online."

I ask Sammie if I can stay over, and of course she says yes. I decide not to bother texting my mom to tell her. I'm supposed to take Mila to camp tomorrow morning before I come back for my morning shift, but I figure if she cares enough, she'll find me.

I don't sleep well anymore. I can't remember the last time I had a really good night. Even when I do sleep, I feel like I'm half-awake, my dreams filled with running and reading and testing and failing. Crowds watching me. Naked dreams. Dreams that are predictable and boring, and yet interminable and torturous.

The morning light is filtering in through the blinds, and I'm already awake, but I'm still startled when Sammie sits up in bed. "Oh my God. Wake. Up."

She's on her phone. "Ohmygodohmygodohmygod. Evan. Just. Messaged. Me."

"What are you talking about?"

"Through Instagram. Look." She holds up her phone to my face and I have to let my eyes focus before I can really see what it is that she's showing me. It's a photo of the back of his hand with a phone number written on it. "His number," she says. "He sent it to me privately."

I sit up to look at her bedside clock. "Why is he sending you messages at six-thirty A.M.?"

"I just posted a pic from yesterday—my Marilyn photos, you know? I couldn't think of a good caption, so I waited until just now to post—and then he messaged me right after."

"Good! That's great," I say, but it's not great. It's weird and awkward, and I don't know why I blurt that out.

I mean, he's flirting with her. He responded to a half-naked photo of her with his phone number. It's what she wanted. And I need to remember that as good as I felt in that crazy, wonderful moment yesterday, I don't want him. Life is complicated enough as it is. And I want Sammie to be happy.

"He wants me to text him."

"So, text him, then."

"Okay. Yeah. Yeah? Okay. I'll do it."

She hovers over her phone and sends him a message. I don't ask what it says. I lie back down.

She lies back next to me. "Okay. I sent it. Oh God. I can't believe it."

"Did he say anything else with the picture?"

"No. It's just his number. I hope it was meant for me. Maybe it wasn't meant for me?"

"It was meant for you."

Her phone lights up. She reads the message and nearly wakes the whole building with her squeal. "HE WANTS TO COME OVER!"

"Wait. What? Here? Now?"

"Yes." She ignores my questions while she types something back to him and then throws the cover off our legs. "He's riding his bike over from campus. Come on. Get up. We've got to get ourselves together. Will you fix my hair? Maybe that cool braid again? I've got to put on some lipstick or something. He's going to be here in ten minutes."

"Why?"

"I don't know. He says he needs us for something."

"He knows I'm here?"

"Yes, I told him." And then it hits me at the same time it hits her. "Maybe he just wants to see you."

She's right. She's totally and completely right. This is the point where I should admit it all. I should tell her that he kissed me—that I kissed him.

But I don't. Instead, I insist that's not what it is, because I can't let it go any further. "He messaged *you*," I say. "He texted *you*."

"Yeah, okay. You're right."

We get ourselves dressed quietly so as not to wake her mom, who probably came home around two, like usual. I braid Sammie's hair and then sit on her bed while she works her makeup magic in her mirror: foundation, eyeliner, mascara, lipstick, the works.

I throw my hair in a ponytail and put on my bra.

Her phone buzzes, and she checks it. "He's downstairs," she says.

She tells the doorman to send him up. A few minutes later, there's a soft, rhythmic knock at the door.

"He's here." She looks terrified.

"So answer it."

"Yes. Okay. I'll answer it."

I follow her down the hallway and through the empty living room. She opens the door. Evan's standing there, clearly upset.

He doesn't say hi or anything—there are no formal greetings, no pleasantries or salutations. He walks past us and sits on the couch. "I need your help. Professor Cox needs your help. He's in trouble. Deep trouble." He's breathless and upset.

"Shhh," Sammie says. "My mom's sleeping. Come on. Let's go up to the roof."

Sammie leads us out the door, and we follow her toward the elevator. Evan looks at me, and I have to look away, for fear of acknowledging what happened yesterday. He reaches for my hand to try to hold it, but I pull back and shake my head.

Sammie turns and asks, "What's going on?"

"Nothing!" I say.

This confuses Sammie. "What? What are you talking about?"

"What? Oh, you mean with Professor Cox? Yeah—" I try to recover. "What's going on, Evan?"

The elevator door opens. "I'll tell you when we get upstairs," Evan says. "I'll explain everything. Or at least I'll try to."

Inside the elevator, the air between us is thick. We're all facing one another, our backs against the mirrored wall, and it's so incredibly awkward. Sammie looks at Evan, and then Evan looks at me. I try my best to keep my attention on the numbers that rise one by one as the elevator takes us up to the roof.

Finally, the elevator door opens. We follow Sammie out, and she uses her keys to unlock the fire door.

We walk through the party room and exit onto the roof. The sky is dark and blue in the west, while Lake Michigan, in the east, is lit up orange from the rising sun. Below us the city is not quite awake. There's a weird silence in the air, and I'm not sure if it's because of Evan or if it's something else completely.

At first, we try to sit down on the benches, but they're wet with dew, so we just lean against the railing and look out at the sunrise. It's early Monday morning, and most Bennett residents are on their way to work. Even my mom must be up already, getting Mila ready for camp. I probably should go down and let her know I'm with Sammie. But I figure if she were really worried, she would have texted Sammie already.

"Professor Cox called me last night. He's in jail. Someone called after that tomato stunt. I was his one phone call. He needs my help."

"What tomato stunt?" Sammie asks.

Evan fills her in on what happened yesterday.

"I can't believe I missed it," Sammie says. "What does he want from you?"

"Well, first, to make sure his dog is okay. And something about clearing out some things. Some incriminating things, maybe?"

"That's why you came here?" Sammie asks, clearly disappointed that he hasn't come for her. "To convince us to do what, exactly?"

"Honestly? Nothing. I just needed to get into the building. And now that I'm in, I don't really need you to do anything, I guess. He said there's a key under the mat, and technically, I could just go in myself." And then he says, "But I'd like for you guys to come with me."

"Okay," Sammie says quickly. "I'm in."

I know Sammie doesn't want me here, so this should be the perfect excuse to say no, but I'm worried that if I leave Evan and Sammie alone together, he'll tell her about our kiss.

"Ugh," I say. "Really? We're really doing this?"

"Don't you want to prove to Professor Harold Joseph Cox that there's love in the world? I mean, he reached out for help, and we need to show him that there are good people like us who could love him."

"And destroy evidence for him?"

"Yes." Evan laughs quietly. "And destroy evidence for him."

"Fantastic," I say. "This is exactly what I want to be doing on a beautiful summer's morning. Sneaking into odd men's apartments and committing possibly illegal but ultimately altruistic acts of deception."

The building, with its skeleton of concrete and steel, breathes heavily against the push of the elevator's descent. There's a constant hum of air—it sweeps up through the elevator shaft as we descend toward the eleventh floor—it's louder than usual, maybe because we're not stopping at multiple floors to pick up more passengers. Or maybe it's because we're all quiet and nervous, and it's even more awkward and weird between us now. Along with the loud hum of the building I hear the beating of my own heart inside my head.

The doors open to the silent and empty hallway.

"Professor Cox said it's eleven eighteen," Evan says.

"This way," Sammie says. "He's kitty-corner from you. Right, Vivi?"

"Let's see, if I'm in sixteen twenty-two—" We walk to 1118. "Then yes, he'd be two over in this direction."

A door opens down the hall and a mom with a kid in a stroller emerges, the kid in full tantrum mode, crying and screaming for his pacifier. She gives us a suspicious look, like she knows we don't belong here.

Rather than stopping at Professor Cox's door, Sammie and I follow Evan as he continues walking down the hall. "Did we get off at the wrong floor?" he says, and then we follow him into the emergency stairwell.

We wait there for a few minutes until we hear the ding and the shutting elevator doors, which drown out the wailing kid's cries.

Evan sneaks a peak into the hallway. "All clear," he says. We follow him to number 1118.

Evan bends down to look for the key, which Professor Cox said was under the mat. We hear sniffing from behind the door. "Must be his dog," I say, and then he starts barking and scraping. "Is it there?"

"Got it," Evan says. He stands up and holds out a gold key. "Here we go."

He puts the key in the lock and turns. The door opens. The dog jumps at our feet, and his barking echoes through the hallway even louder now. "Quick, get in." Evan bends down and picks him up. "Shhh, boy. It's okay. Everything's okay now."

Sammie and I follow Evan inside, and I shut the door.

I expected the smell of dog, but instead I'm hit by the thick, sharp smell of incense—patchouli and orange. Even from Sammie's apartment, we could only really see the front room, the dining room, where his cactuses are. I also expected a bizarre dungeon of a room, but when I step inside, I'm shocked by the emptiness of it. It's a small studio apartment that's decorated all in white, like a hospital room. There's a small white futon that looks like it serves as his bed, with neatly folded sheets and blankets on the table next to it. Apart from the dining room table, there's not much else—just a desk with some papers scattered on top and a small white bookshelf with a few dozen books stacked in piles.

"It's like he just moved in," Sammie says.

"Or is about to move out," I say.

Evan picks up Professor Cox's shivering dog in his arms. He takes the dog to the kitchen, where he pours out some food and water. "He already went on the floor," he calls. "Poor guy. We'll need to take him out."

"Does he have a name?"

"His dog tag says 'Peyton Manning.' Never would have taken Professor Cox for a Broncos fan." The dog takes a break from drinking his water to lick Evan's hand. "But he's cute."

I walk around the apartment and try to figure out what it is, exactly, we're searching for. On the walls are a few of his paintings and some framed photos of Professor Cox posing with his dog, and I have to admit, it's really sweet, but also really sad. There are no photos of him with anyone else. I wonder who the photographer was.

Sammie runs to the closet. "Let's look for the bathing suits!"

"How about we just take care of his dog," I say. "And then let's get out of here?"

"Found them!" Sammie's standing at the open closet, and there they are: a few dozen bathing suits, each on a hanger.

"Unbelievable." I turn to Evan. "What, exactly, are we supposed to be looking for?"

He shrugs. "Honestly, I'm not sure. Something he's worried about the police finding? Anything that looks weird or suspicious, I guess?"

"All I see are clothes. And shoes. And bathing suits. Lots and lots of bathing suits."

The dog emerges from the kitchen and runs straight to Evan. Evan picks him up and takes him over to the desk. "What have we got here, boy?" Evan shuffles through a stack of postcards. "Oh no . . . take a look at this."

Sammie and I walk over and each of us picks up a batch to skim through. They're notes, postmarked and sent via USPS.

All addressed to Professor Cox, from Petyon Manning—the Chihuahua, not the football player.

"I didn't realize it was so bad," Evan says. Some are notes, little philosophical musings about "idealism" and "materialism," which are vaguely familiar to me from my history classes, and then other notes on "reflexivity" and "agency," which I've never heard of before. Then there are the orders, written from his dog, telling him to do things. They're harmless reminders to pay the electric bill and do the laundry, but there are quite possibly hundreds of these postcards. It doesn't seem like it's something that was done for fun.

"This doesn't prove or disprove anything, really," I say.

Sammie heads toward the balcony. "Maybe it's something in his paintings. I'll check out here."

"I'll check the bathroom," I say.

"Good idea," Evan says. The dog barks, and Evan picks him up. "Come on, boy."

I did not mean for him to follow me, but it's done. I walk into the bathroom, Evan behind me, that silly dog panting in his arms.

Evan closes the door partway and puts the dog down. I open the cabinet door and find it near empty, a toothbrush and toothpaste, deodorant, and Tylenol. "Nothing here," I say.

Evan puts his hand on my shoulder, and I turn toward him. "Can I kiss you?" He whispers this. "I'd like to kiss you again."

I want to say no. First of all, Sammie's in the other room. Plus, this is all so weird and complicated, standing in some man's apartment, searching for something—I don't even know what.

But then I don't say no. I don't say anything. Instead, I stand there, silent and still. And I lean up to him. And we kiss.

Again.

"Viviana!" It's Sammie, calling from the other room. "Viviana, I think—I think you need to come here."

"Oh, no." I step back away from him.

"What's wrong?"

Sammie calls out to me again. "Vivi, quick!"

"I'm sorry." I shake my head. "I can't do this."

I leave Evan in the bathroom and I want to run out of the apartment, but Sammie's calling for me to come to the window.

"What's going on?"

"Vivi, it's—" She points outside. "It's your dad."

"What are you talking about? My dad's in Singapore."

Sammie shakes her head. "He's right there. On your balcony."

I look up out the window toward my apartment, and she's right. It is my dad. Not in Singapore. He's here. He's home.

Why is he home?

I head toward the balcony. I'm too excited. I'm not sure if he'll be able to hear me, but I'll call for him. Maybe he's going to surprise us.

As I step out on the balcony, I'm hit by a warm gust of air—it's early morning, but it's warming up already. I can't help but think that my dad should change out of his suit, that he's going to be too hot today.

I'm about to call out to him, but he's on the phone.

His words float down to me before I can call out to him.

"No, honey . . . I'm sorry. . . . I love you, too. . . . Yes, Paige, I told you I'd be home this week, but they need me here longer. . . . When I get back, I'll take you out. . . . I promise. . . . Paige, listen—"

Paige? Who's Paige?

"Yes, a special date, just you and me . . . like we used to. . . . Yes, in the beginning."

Who is he talking to?

"Yes, Paige, I love you, too. . . . I always have. . . . Yes, more than anything. More than ever."

Oh my God. What is happening?

The words register, one by one.

The truth swells over me.

The truth about why he's leaving. Or rather, why he left. Why he disappeared and my mom's back in school and why no one's explained anything about anything.

The city sways below me. I could fall into it, into the reality that is my life.

"Vivi? Are you okay?" Sammie's leaning out the door.

I look at her and shake my head.

"What's going on?"

"I can't be out here right now."

"Okay." She reaches her hand out to me, and I take it.

I step inside, into her arms.

But then I pull back.

"I kissed Evan," I say. "And he kissed me. I'm sorry. I'm so sorry, Sammie."

"Wait . . . what? What are you talking about? When did you kiss Evan?"

"Yesterday. At the pool. After you left."

"Before I told you I was over him?"

I nod. "And again. Just now in the bathroom. Oh God—" I feel like I need to sit down. I reach out to her, but she pulls away. "Sammie, I'm so very sorry. I don't want to hurt anyone anymore."

I say this, but it's too late. Her face changes. She sees me now for what I am. Whereas a minute ago she was my only friend, I can see that, here, now that I see the truth of what I am and where I came from, I am nothing but her ultimate pain and betrayal.

Just like my dad.

"Nice," she says. "Real nice. You know how much I like him. I thought I could trust you."

"You can, Sammie. You can—"

But then she turns away from me and starts running toward the door. She's stopped by Evan, who emerges from the bathroom, two pill bottles in each hand.

"I think I found it," he says. "I think I found what he doesn't want anyone to know."

"I could really care less," she says. And then she runs past him, out the door. Behind her, Professor Cox's dog barks at her ankles and then moans when the door slams.

Evan looks at me, confused. "What was that about?"

"Nothing." The dog comes up to me and barks at my feet.

I feel sick. Nauseous. Dizzy.

"Is everything okay?"

"No," I choke out. "It's not."

Evan walks toward me and reaches out to touch my arm.

I step back. "Please don't touch me."

"Okay . . ."

"And please don't kiss me. No more. Not ever again."

"You kissed me."

"I know. I did. And I shouldn't have. I can't do this. I shouldn't have done this."

"Is this about Sammie?"

"Yes—no. I mean, it is. And it's not. It's just—I need to get out of here."

I run out of the apartment, half-hoping to find Sammie in the hallway so I can beg for forgiveness, half-hoping she's gone so I don't have to face her.

The hallway is empty. I can't go back to my apartment. I can't face my dad.

I can't call Sammie, and I can't go back to Evan.

I take the emergency stairs all the way down to the lobby. I exit the building.

The city has woken up. The sidewalks are bustling with businesspeople, families, kids.

They're all spinning around me. Spiraling around me.

I can't pass out again. I can't end up in the ER again.

I crouch down on a curb and try to breathe. I'm stuck, in the middle of the sidewalk, crying, sobbing, heaving for breath. I can feel passersby giving me funny looks, so I wipe my face and start walking.

But I don't know where to go.

I have nowhere to go.

I have no one to go to.

PART THREE

Viviana Rabinovich-Lowe's College Application Checklist

☐ ~~May: AP Exams~~ *bombed*

☐ ~~June–July: Design and Engineering Summer Academy~~ *thwarted*
☐ ~~July: Work on College Apps~~
☐ August: ~~Work on College Apps;~~ Study for SAT

☐ September: Finalize Stanford Application

     Take
☐ October: SAT General Test;
   Submit Early Action Application to Stanford

SAT Math: Sample Question

A researcher wants to know if there is an association between lies, heartbreak, and life suckage for the population of sixteen-year-olds in the United States. After conducting a broad survey, which of the following conclusions is most relevant to this study?

(A) Girls who fall for cute guys despite their best intentions experience the most major life suckage.

(B) Girls who kiss their best friend's crushes and then lie about it experience the most major life suckage.

(C) Girls who discover their fathers are involved with other women mere months after leaving their families experience the most major life suckage.

(D) Girls with broken hearts experience the most major life suckage.

(E) All of the above.

The Fourth of July is one hundred times worse than Memorial Day. Maybe it's because I have to work every day this weekend. Maybe it's because Sammie's requested a shift change, and so now I'm on the desk by myself. Or maybe it's because it's 102 degrees, which means that everyone in Bennett Village is here, and they can't understand why there aren't enough umbrellas, or why we've run out of Diet Coke, or why it's taking me so long to record their visitor passes. Or maybe, as usual, the answer is all of the above.

I wish I could quit. After that day on the balcony in Professor Cox's apartment, I tried to tell my mom that I wanted to stay home after all. She asked me if I'd been having more panic attacks, sort of accusing me of having them, not asking out of a real sense of concern. So I rescinded my request.

And I said no.

Which is a complete and utter lie.

Ever since that day, the heart palpitations and choking feeling have been constant. And I've had two more Episodes in the middle of the night. But I didn't wake her. I didn't want to end up back at the hospital for something I knew would pass eventually.

When she persisted in asking me why I wanted to quit, and I didn't have a good answer, she just shrugged and said,

"If you are not sick, I see no reason for you to quit. It's an easy job and decent money."

So I'm here all weekend.

And it's full life suckage.

Vanessa joins me behind the desk and scans the ID of a resident who's been complaining, rather loudly, the whole time she's been in line about how she's "melting in this heat" and how "this is taking forever."

"Thank you," I whisper after the woman is gone. "She's been giving me the side-eye the whole time she's been in line."

"People are jerks," Vanessa says while swiping more IDs. "Where's Sammie?"

"I don't know."

"You guys aren't scheduled together anymore?"

"Guess not," I say with a shrug.

"Had a fight?"

"Something like that."

"I'm sorry," Vanessa says. "That blows. Hope you guys make up soon."

I don't say anything.

"Do you have any plans for tonight? Any parties?"

This city loves a party. Summer in Chicago means concerts, parades, and street fairs. Fireworks shows at Navy Pier two times a week. Taste of Chicago, with its rows and rows of restaurant fare. Normally, I love a party, too, especially for the Fourth of July weekend, which has always been when Mila and I celebrate our birthdays. Every year on Saturday night, we have a small party. Mila invites a few of her friends, and we have a rooftop barbecue, with my dad cooking hot dogs and hamburgers on the grill, and then we watch the fireworks show from the roof, all of Mila's little friends oohing and aahing at the explosions. I only invite Sammie, so it's not really a party for me, but Mila demands that my name be on the cake, too. We're always together.

We haven't planned anything this year. Mila said she doesn't want one, since Dad's not here. When I asked my mom what we should do for Mila, she recommended that I bring her down for an afternoon swim so she could put some streamers around our apartment for a little afternoon surprise party.

She didn't say anything about my birthday.

I don't really feel like celebrating anything anyway. In addition to our birthdays, we're supposed to be celebrating independence and the pursuit of happiness, but I feel anything but free, anything but happy. I am trapped in this knot of isolation and lies and secrets. I can hardly even look my mom in the eye without wanting to cry. I thought I could never experience shame worse than what I experienced with Dean, but knowing my father is already with another woman somehow feels a thousand times worse.

"No plans," I say. "At least not yet," I add, so as not to sound completely lame.

I think maybe she's going to invite me to do something, but I'm not really in the mood to go out, even if it is the night before my birthday.

Instead, Vanessa tells me that she has to go to a barbecue

on the North Side. "It's going to be boring. Just my family, hanging out on lawn chairs, eating cheap hot dogs and watching the fireworks."

I don't say anything in response. I don't say how perfect that sounds, or how much I miss cheap hot dogs and fireworks and boring family parties.

Instead, I turn my attention to the next family in line and scan their IDs.

I clock out and head upstairs to get Mila. I expect her to be panting at the door, raring to go, but instead, she's slumped on the couch, watching *National Geographic* and sucking on her pinkie. My mom's at the dining room table, working on the computer, as usual.

"Happy day, birthday girl!" I force this out, and then pick up the remote and click off the TV. "Are you excited to be going swimming?"

Mila leans toward me, takes the remote from my hand, and turns the TV back on. "No."

"No? What's wrong?"

"You know what's wrong. Daddy's not here."

"I know," I mumble. I try to take the remote from her hands, but she holds on tight. "I'm sorry. But don't you want to go to the pool? We can still celebrate your special day!"

She puts her pinkie finger in her mouth and sucks on it. I haven't seen her do this in years.

"Come on, Mila. I'm going to get my suit on. I'll take you out for ice cream after."

My mom looks up from her computer. "Yes, Mila. You have to go." My mom winks at me. "I have a conference call I have to take, and I need the apartment to myself."

"But it's my birthday and I want to be with you." Mila starts to cry. "I don't understand why you have to have a call on a Saturday. On my birthday? I mean, why do you have to work so much?"

I think that maybe my mom will bust out with the truth that she's just trying to get us out of the apartment because she has a surprise for Mila, but she sticks to the story. "I'm sorry, Mila. I have certain responsibilities. One day you will understand. One day you will have to act like a grown-up, too."

This seems harsh. I want to call my mom out on her unnecessary guilt trips, especially on Mila's birthday, but I figure it will just lead to another fight, and the only thing I can really work on right now is getting Mila down to the pool.

"Come on, Mila. We'll go down for a little bit, and then when we come back upstairs, maybe there'll be a surprise for you."

That perks her up. She takes her finger out from the corner of her mouth. "What kind of surprise?"

"Well, it wouldn't be a surprise if I told you. Now go get your suit on!"

Mila jumps off the couch, runs to her room, and reappears in less than two minutes fully decked out in her purple bikini, goggles, a snorkel, and flip-flops.

We head downstairs and snag a shady spot next to a potted plant.

"Is Evan here?" Mila asks as I spray her with sunscreen. "Are you going to kiss him again?"

"What are you talking about? I've never kissed him."

"Yes you did. That day during the tomato attack. You kissed him while we were under the umbrella."

"I—how—how did you see that?"

"I'm not blind, you know."

"Well—turn around, let me spray your back—I haven't kissed him since and I'm not going to kiss him again. Anyway, it's none of your business."

"I like Evan." Mila peers around toward the pool. "Is he here?"

"Yeah, probably somewhere." He was working earlier when I was here, but we didn't speak to each other, partly because it was so busy, and partly because I've put up a wall that he knows not to cross.

Since that day in Professor Cox's apartment, I've had only a few days when Evan's been working, and each time, he's tried to talk to me with whispered apologies and questions.

As he leaned over the desk to grab his whistle: "I didn't realize Sammie liked me."

While I swept the deck: "I'm so sorry you guys aren't talking now."

As I counted money: "Why won't you talk to me?"

From his chair while he was on duty: "Aren't you at all curious about Professor Cox?"

As we passed in the hallway by the equipment room: "Can't we even be friends?"

At first, I didn't say anything. I just stared at him until

he backed off. But finally, after he asked that last question, I responded with a quick reminder that it's none of my business—not Professor Cox, not Sammie, not his desire for friendship. "Can't you please just leave me alone?"

And since then, he has. For a good week, he hasn't asked any more questions. I still feel his gaze sometimes, while we're talking in groups, or if he comes into the office when I'm there. But he doesn't talk to me anymore.

"Okay, okay, I'm covered." Mila steps away from me and the sunscreen bottle. "The sun's going down anyway. Can we go in already?"

She runs away from me toward the water. I spray myself as quickly as I can and follow her. Mila's at the foot of the lifeguard chair, where Evan is on duty. Vanessa's sitting at the edge of the pool, dangling her feet in the water.

"You're back!" Vanessa says to me. "I thought you were gone for the night."

"It's Mila's birthday, and she wanted to go swimming."

"I didn't want to go swimming." Mila crosses her arms across her chest and pouts. "I wanted to sit on the couch and watch my program."

"You'd rather watch TV than swim?" Vanessa asks.

"It was *National Geographic*. They were talking about how there's a kind of moth that lays its eggs in sloth poop. They have a symbiotic relationship. It's gross but also cool."

"Symbiotic?" Vanessa asks. "How old is she?"

"I'm nine today!" Mila says, beaming. And then she looks up at Evan. "Hi, Evan!"

Evan keeps his eyes on the pool, which is packed with kids.

"Will you play Marco Polo with us again today?" Mila calls up to him.

"Wish I could," Evan says without looking down at us. "I have to work."

Mila pouts and drops her shoulders.

"I'll play with you," Vanessa says.

This appeases Mila, and we all jump in.

I dive underwater, and when I come up, I can't help but look over at Evan to see if he's looking my way like that day in June.

He's not.

I'm not sure if I'm relieved or disappointed.

Mila splashes water in my face. "You're it, Vivi!"

I close my eyes and reach out to play the game.

Habits of an Effective Test Taker #4

What if you aren't familiar with the topic, and you aren't sure which is the best possible answer? One helpful strategy is to eliminate the extremes that are obviously wrong, and then take your best guess. This gives you higher odds of getting the question right.

Vanessa joins us for our celebratory ice cream at Scoop Heaven, this little place at the edge of Bennett Village, and then Mila and I head back up to our apartment. She's busting to see the surprise. And after getting two texts, first at 6:45 and again at 7:15, from my mom telling me not to come back yet because she wasn't ready, I have to say my curiosity is firmly piqued. Streamers shouldn't take that long.

We open the door, to find the entire apartment filled with

not only streamers but dozens of balloons, and there's a giant cake that my mom's now lighting with candles. I search the apartment for the extra surprise—the one that's supposed to be for me—but I don't see anything unusual beyond the fact that my mom really did go crazy with the decorations, and I'm not sure how we're going to eat all that cake.

Mila is jumping up and down with excitement, her previous complaints silenced for good. That smile is there again on my mom's face. It's good to see. She begins to sing "Happy Birthday," and she motions for me to join in.

So I do, and Mila's beaming with excitement. She loves this attention from our mom—she's been desperately craving it for months.

We sing the last line—and that's when the surprise appears.

My father.

He steps out from the hallway and sings the last line with us.

He's standing there with a huge, cocky smile on his face, singing as if he hasn't been gone for nearly six months, as if he never left.

Mila runs to him and wraps her arms around his waist. He hugs her tight and then lifts her up into his arms. "Daddy! Daddy!" Mila yells. "You're the best surprise of all!"

"Quick," he says, putting her down. "Blow out your candles before they melt into the frosting."

I look at my mom. Her smile is weak and strained. It's not like the one she was wearing before.

I feel sick.

"Viviana," she says coldly, "say hello to your father."

I don't move.

I can't move.

My dad puts Mila down and looks at me. He opens his arms, as though I'm just going to walk into them. As if the past six months haven't happened. As if he hasn't already moved on from us. As if he hasn't been living a lie.

"Come, now, Viviana," my mom says, her voice softening. "Your father is home now—with us. He is home now, for good. Everything is fine."

She doesn't know the reality of the situation. She can't see the real answer—that he's a liar, a cheat, a complete and utter weasel. She thinks this was just a fight—nothing more—and she thinks he's going to move back and we're all going to be okay.

My head is dizzy with this terrible surprise.

I wonder how much she knows. Or doesn't know.

They are looking at me and waiting for me to say something, to do something, to walk into my father's arms and trust him again.

I see the choice that I have: Pretend that I don't know the truth, embrace him, welcome him home. Or say something: ask him where he's been for six months, ask him why he suddenly wants to be with us again, demand that he tell my mom and Mila about Paige, about his other life, the one where he loves some woman named Paige and we don't exist.

Mila runs over to me and pulls at my arm. "Viviana," she whines. "It's Daddy. He's home."

I don't have this choice now. Not in front of Mila. Not on her birthday.

I walk up to my father.

I wrap my left arm around his waist and I force out the word: "Hi."

"Where's my hug?" he asks before sweeping me up into his arms. I let him squeeze me, but I don't return the hug. He puts me down and steps back. "You've gotten taller, I think." He looks at Mila. "Both of you."

"We haven't seen you since January," I say. "That's six months."

"Viviana, be nice," my mom says.

"I know," he says. "And I'm so sorry I had to be gone so much." He doesn't say anything about the separation. The almost divorce. I look over at my mom.

She motions for us to sit at the table, which is set with the good china, the dishes we never use, the ones they received as a wedding present. "Let's just sit. I've made a stuffed chicken and noodles, and then we'll eat some cake."

My father takes his seat at the head of the table.

I sit down at the opposite end, far away from him.

Mila moves her chair so that it's close to my dad. My mom brings in the food from the kitchen.

He looks at me across the table. "How's the new job?"

"It's fine," I say.

"She works too much," my mom says. "She's supposed to be resting."

"Mama, I'm fine."

My dad frowns. "You made a promise to your mother—"

"I said I'm fine. Would you just let me be—"

"No!" Mila yells. "Stop it! There's no arguing today. It's

my birthday, and I made a wish that there would be no more arguing. So stop it. All of you." She's on the verge of tears, but she's not crying. Not yet.

"Okay, Mila," my father says. "We're sorry." He looks at my mom and me. "We're all sorry, right?"

"Yes." I nod. "I'm sorry, Mila."

"You're right," my mom agrees, finally taking her seat. "Let's eat now."

We are silent for a few minutes, except for the sounds of my mom dishing out noodles onto her plate and Mila choking back tears.

I can feel it. I am struggling against an Episode. I want to cry, too—to cry and collapse and scream. But I can't. Not now.

I can't eat, so I take a few sips of water.

Mila gives me a funny look, like she knows what's happening inside my mind and she's daring me to try to stir it all up again.

Finally, my father pulls out a stuffed lion he brought back for Mila from Singapore, and Mila is distracted and fine again. She jumps into his lap and she's smiling and laughing and snuggling against him, her new toy in her arms.

I ask to be excused for a minute. I head into my room, where I collapse onto my bed. I breathe and breathe and breathe, slow and steady, like the doctors told me to. It works. My head settles and my bones turn solid once more.

I have to be okay tonight.

I have to.

For Mila.
She made a wish.

Mila doesn't get to sleep until nearly midnight, what with our father's return and the sugar rush from her three pieces of cake and the excitement of the fireworks. She begged my parents to take her up to the roof so she could see them better, and when I asked (politely, I thought) if I could stay downstairs by myself, my mom gave me a look of death. I acquiesced, quite unwillingly, and then all night, my father kept asking me, "Are you okay, Vivi?" And then Mila would prod me: "Why aren't you smiling, Vivi? It's my birthday. Yours, too, tomorrow. And Daddy's here. Please smile, Vivi. Why aren't you okay?"

Now the city's quiet, and Mila's asleep. I'm alone in my room, finally.

I shut off the lights and crawl under my covers.

I let the day rush over me.

I try to make the tears come, and to let myself cry, but I can't scream into the pillow like I want, I can't sob like I want, or they'll all come running in here asking if I'm okay.

I desperately want to text Sammie.

I desperately want to run upstairs to her room.

I miss her so much.

My father knocks at my door. "Viviana? Can I come in?"

I catch my breath and hold it. The door's locked. If I am quiet enough, he'll think I'm asleep and leave me alone.

"Viviana?"

I hold my breath.

"Let me in, please."

No. Go away.

"Your mother and I have to tell you something, before tomorrow. Before Mila wakes up."

Leave me alone.

"We need to talk. An honest talk."

He hooks me. I want an honest talk.

I let out my breath and open the door.

"Are you okay?"

"Would you please stop asking me that? I think the answer's pretty obvious."

"Fair enough," he says. He pushes his glasses up on his face and looks away from me.

I'm making him nervous.

Good.

"Come in the living room for a few minutes?"

I follow him. My mom's sitting on the couch, a pillow held against her chest. My dad sits down next to her, and she places her head against his shoulder.

"So you guys are back together now? No divorce?"

My mom lifts her head. "Please, Viviana, lower your voice. Mila—"

My father pats the couch next to him. "Please come sit down here."

I ignore his request and lean on the armrest of the recliner instead.

"What's going on?"

He puts his arms around my mom, but instead of softening into him, she stiffens. "We are trying to work things out," he says.

"Why couldn't we have had this conversation with Mila?"

"Because we figured you might have questions," my mom says. "Questions about what's happened that maybe we couldn't answer in front of Mila."

I do have questions. So many questions. He said we were going to have an honest talk, and now's my chance to lay all my cards on the table.

But I don't know where to start.

"So that means you're here now?" I sputter out. "For good?"

"No," he says. "Only for a few weeks. And then I'm back to Singapore. But only for a month this time."

"I thought you were trying to work things out."

"I still have a job."

"And we still have bills to pay," my mom says.

"Does Mila know that?"

"Not yet."

"But she thinks you're here for good."

My father nods. "We'll tell her first thing tomorrow morning."

I want to ask all my questions. They run through my head. Do you know about her, Mama? Are you done sleeping around, Dad? Who is this Paige, this other woman in your life? Why are we everything to you *now*? Why weren't we everything to you before? How am I supposed to trust you?

My questions are on the tip of my tongue.

I could tell them what I heard—what I know.

He inches toward me and reaches for my arm. "I've come to realize that you three matter to me more than anything."

His words to Paige echo: *more than anything.*

The room spins.

I could tell her now. I should tell her now.

My mom looks at my father. "We are trying to save twenty years of our lives together."

I want to cry, to scream, to yell, to wake up Mila, to wake up the entire building, to shout the truth about his horrible, cruel lie to anyone who will listen. I want my mother to know that she's been tricked—we all have.

I look at her. She whispers, through her tears, "We love you both so very much."

I can't do it. I can't hurt her, and I can't hurt Mila. If they find out, their entire lives will be destroyed.

I stand up, and my father stands up, too, thinking he's going to be able to give me another awkward hug. But I don't let him. Instead, I run to my room.

I lock the door and collapse on my bed.

I hear my parents' whispers in the hallway, my name, Mila's name—they hover by my door, and then they walk away.

I can't breathe.

I can't breathe.

I can't breathe.

Slowly, slowly, the darkness settles me. I listen to my parents' night noises and finally I am calmed by the silence of a sleeping apartment. I lie on my back and take control of my breath. With each inhale, I see it all: my father for what he is, my mother for how she tries, Mila for everything she wants from us.

I've already learned what it means to hurt someone I love.

I will never do it again.

Habits of an Effective Test Taker #5

Trust your first impressions. The first answer that comes to mind is often the correct one.

I can't fall asleep. It's 4:00 A.M. I've tried reading, staring out the window, writing five texts to Sammie that I ended up not sending, and looking up Evan's Instagram account because when you're on the verge of a full-blown Episode in the middle of the night, all rational thoughts are meaningless, and even guilt isn't enough to stop you from doing stupid things.

I can't toss and turn anymore, so I finally get out of bed. I head to the kitchen to make myself some toast. I figure I'll watch TV on mute to see if that will help me fall asleep. And if I don't fall asleep, I'll just suck it up and be tired at work later. I've gone days without sleeping before. I'll just make sure not to get on any bicycles.

I'm about to spread jam on my toast when I see it.

My dad's phone.

It lights up and buzzes.

Someone's texting him in the middle of the night.

I reach for it.

Fortunately, my dad doesn't have a pass code on his phone. For someone who likes to lie so much, he really should.

I slide the phone open and open his messages. There it is. A message from Paige. More Than Anything Paige.

Can't sleep. Too excited to see you tomorrow. 6:00 P.M., right?

And then a second text:

The kids can't wait, either. All day they kept asking if Daddy will bring them toys, but I know they really just want YOU here.

And then a third:

You've been gone too long these past few months. We need to talk. I know you don't want to hear it, but it's hard. I will go back to work if it means you finally coming home for good.

And finally:

*Please let's talk? I know you're awake. Your secretary said
you were on your way to the airport. Talk to me, Benjamin.*

She thinks he's in Singapore.

She thinks he's her husband.

She thinks he's the father of her kids.

She doesn't know about us.

The toaster dings and snaps me out of my shock, but not
soon enough. The bread is completely burned and the
kitchen stinks.

I shut off his phone and run to my room.

I text Sammie.

Please can I come over? My life is falling apart.

I press SEND, but I don't wait for her response.

I throw on my gym shoes, grab my mom's keys, and run
out of the apartment.

My phone vibrates.

Of course.

It's Sammie. I never should have texted her. I should
throw my phone off this roof.

A few minutes later: *Where are you?*

Where am I?

I am thirty-eight stories into the sky. There are stars
here. I am on my back, falling into this hard, damp floor. I

close my eyes, and the words are there in the dark of my lids. I am spinning below them.

My mom just got home, but she's asleep. Come upstairs.

There is a hot wind. There is the weight of rain, not yet here. A heavy pressure of water coming.

I'm at the door. I'm waiting for you.

The words of this other woman. The real truth of her life. Of his life. The words are there in the dark of my lids.

I'm here. Where are you?

Breathe, Viviana. Breathe yourself out. Breathe yourself out of this spinning place.

The words are still there when I open my eyes.

You matter.

More than anything.

All of it: lies.

Sammie finds me. I don't know how she does it again, how she knows, but she finds me on the roof, and she leads me back to her place, where she tucks me into her bed. She brings me water and feeds me cookies and sits with me until I'm ready to talk.

"What's going on?"

I shake my head. I'm not ready.

"Do you want to cry?"

"No."

"Do you want another cookie?"

"No."

"Let me know if there's anything else you need."

"Okay."

She plays with her phone while I stare out the window. It's my birthday today. I'm seventeen. One more year until I'm eighteen. One more long year before I can leave this terrible place and get away from my selfish, irresponsible parents.

"Did you hear about Professor Cox?"

"No."

"Evan didn't tell you?"

I bristle at his name. I don't want to talk about him. I don't want to talk about anything. "He tried," I mutter. "But I didn't let him."

"Oh."

I roll over and look at her. "I'm not going to do that to you anymore."

Sammie puts down her phone and shrugs. "I'm over it. I'm over him."

"What?"

"I can't force someone to like me," she says. "And I don't want to get in the way of someone liking you."

"Come on, Sammie. I'm not choosing a guy over you."

"Well, that's good. I'm glad to hear it. But I want you to know—seriously—I'm really, really over him. If you decide you want to go for Evan again, he's all yours."

"You're way too good to me."

She sits back against the headboard. "Is that why your life is falling apart? Because of Evan?"

"Not at all."

"Do you want to tell me why your life is falling apart yet?"

"No," I say. "But you can tell me about your life. I'd rather hear about you."

"You mean how my mom discovered my Instagram account and how she totally freaked out and made me delete it?"

"Oh, Sammie, no."

"Yeah, no." Her eyes fill up with tears. "I'm not telling you that fun story."

"It's because of me, isn't it?"

"What?"

"She thinks you're going to put up nudie pics like me."

Sammie wipes her eyes and laughs. "Nudie pics?" Then she shrugs. "I don't know. Maybe. Probably. That's not even the half of it."

"I'm sorry."

"Don't be."

I hand her a box of tissues. "What's the other half?"

"Forget the other half. I don't want to talk about it." She blows her nose and clears her throat. "Want to hear about Professor Cox? That's a better story than both yours and mine."

So she tells me. Her mom has been helping him ever since the incident with the tomatoes. It turns out that Professor Cox had been a journalist in the 1960s, a good one who worked for the Associated Press and was on his way to becoming a nationally known writer when he became convinced that he'd caused the Cuban Missile Crisis. He started throwing ashtrays across the office and writing incessantly about all-out nuclear annihilation. At that point, he was diagnosed with schizophrenia, along with some other coexisting issues. He was hospitalized for a while, and after that, and years of medication, he also completed a doctorate in psychology, partly in an attempt to cure himself. He gave most of his inheritance from a family fund to charity. His family, deeply concerned and immensely wealthy, finally stepped in. They connected him with the St. Mary's Seminary, which has parishes in Virginia, where they sent Professor Cox for a "cure of the spirit." But it still wasn't enough to help his mental state, and he went as far as to try to fake his own death.

After that, he was hospitalized again, and this time, he was put on some new meds that actually helped and allowed him to function fairly well. Professor Cox's family donated a good chunk of change to St. Mary's, so they eventually agreed to hire him as a professor. But for the past few years, he'd been trying to self-medicate with some illegal pills. That's what Evan found in his cabinet. That explains the postcards and the tomatoes. "You were right. He does suffer from psychological issues. I feel bad about calling him 'the Nut.'"

"Yeah. Me, too."

"He's back in the hospital, and my mom's been helping to advocate for him. His family's paying her, but I know she's happy to do it."

"Is that why you've been busy with so many errands?"

"Um." Sammie picks up her phone. "Not exactly."

"What do you mean, 'not exactly'?"

"Vivi, forget my stuff. What's going on with you?"

"Ugh." I roll on my back. "You've done such a good job of distracting me. Please don't remind me. What time is it?"

Sammie looks at her phone. "Ten-thirty."

I muffle my face with the pillow. "I don't want to go to work today. I can't go to work today."

"If you tell me what's going on, I'll take your shift."

"If I tell you what's going on with me, will you tell me what's going on with you?"

"No!" Sammie laughs and hits me. "I already said I'd take your shift. If I tell you my stuff, too, it won't be a fair deal!"

"Please, Sammie," I say. "Will you let me be a friend to you? Please?"

Sammie thinks for a moment. "Fine."

"Okay. Good. Thank you."

"Now tell me."

So I do.

I tell her about Mila's surprise gift of my dad's return and the strange midnight conversation with my parents. I tell her about my mom, how she held his hand, how they're promising this honest new life for us. And then I tell her about my father's double life. About Paige and the texts and the kids who are excited about toys from Daddy.

Sammie slides down on the pillow next to mine. "Oh my God, Viviana."

"Yeah."

"You're sure you don't want to cry?"

"No."

And then I look over at her and I see that her pillow is damp. The tears are streaming down her cheeks.

"Why are *you* crying?"

"Because this last year has been so awful for us. For you and me both. We've lost so much." She wipes her eyes.

"Oh." I hadn't really thought about how intertwined our lives have been.

"I'm sorry. I shouldn't be the one crying."

I reach over and give her a hug. "It's okay. One of us should cry. I don't know why I'm not."

"Do you think she knows?"

"My mom? I have no idea."

"Ugh."

"Now you tell me."

"Mine's nothing compared to yours."

"Tell me anyway."

"Well, besides the whole Instagram thing, then this guy I thought I liked has a crush on my best friend, and it turns out they're probably perfect for each other, and so even though my heart is broken, I'm also really happy for them."

I can't help but laugh. "Shut up. Nothing's going to happen. I promise you."

"Sure," she says. "I'll believe it when I see it."

"That's not your news, though. Tell me, for real now."

"Well . . ." Sammie takes a deep breath. "My mom's been interviewing for a new job."

"Okay . . ."

"In Morton Grove."

"Oh."

"We're probably moving there at the end of the summer. We've been looking at apartments. My mom wants to be close to our family."

"No more Uni?"

"Most likely, no. No more Bennett Village. No more Uni."

And that's what makes me cry. I think about my last year of high school without Sammie. I don't know how I'll survive.

I won't.

"Your life really is falling apart," she says. "And so is mine."

Sammie texts Mr. Bautista about our shift change. If we can't be together next year, we can at least, hopefully, be together the rest of the summer. And then we lie in her bed the rest of the morning, both of us crying, blubbering our wet tears into Kleenex, until it's time for her to go take care of my shift.

Habits of an Effective Test Taker #6

On most exams, when you're uncertain of the correct answer, informed guessing can give you an advantage overall.

My parents each text me at least a dozen times, until I finally text them back to let them know that, yes, I'm alive, and, no, I won't be returning home for a while, that I need some space to think, and to please just leave me alone, that it's the only thing I really want for my birthday, to be left alone.

Surprisingly, that makes them stop.

I lie in Sammie's bed alone and think about my dad. I wonder what she looks like—this woman, Paige. She talked about "the kids." Kids. Not just one, but two or maybe more? Like it wasn't an accident. It was planned, thought out, wished for. I try to imagine their faces. I wonder if they have the same red hair that I do and if their eyes are light like mine.

I finally, somehow, drift off into a restless sleep.

I wake up gasping for breath.

I know what I need to do.

I need to see them.

I pick up my phone. It's 4:30 P.M.

Maybe he hasn't left yet. Maybe there's still time.

I grab a shirt and pants out of Sammie's drawer and throw them on. I run down the stairwell and through the lobby, heading toward the corner bus stop across the street from Bennett Tower.

I stand behind the faded glass, and I wait. This woman, Paige, thinks that he's coming home at six, so I hope he hasn't left from our place yet. With any luck, I can catch him.

At twenty past five, he emerges from the lobby of Bennett Tower dressed in a suit and tie, a small duffel bag in his hand. He puts on his sunglasses and starts walking north. I stay on my side of the street, and then I follow him.

My father's always been a fast walker, and I'm trying not to be too obvious in my tracking of him. I do my best to keep a safe distance but also not to stay so far away that I'll lose him. He heads up Clark Street and makes his way into Lincoln Park, where it's harder to stay out of his sight. I slow my pace and almost lose him when he ducks under a bridge and back onto the street. I run after him and catch up enough to be able to follow at a steady pace for another ten minutes or so.

He turns a few corners and walks down some small tree-lined streets, and then finally he arrives at a large and beautiful brownstone on a fancy street named Geneva Terrace. It's three stories high and newly renovated, with a bright red door and perfectly manicured bushes. This other family lives in a giant house on a side street in a much nicer neighborhood than where we live.

He pulls out his key, unlocks the door, and walks inside.

Oh, no.

I wasn't thinking.

I had this vision of him opening the front door and his other wife and his other kids running to him, of him lifting them into his arms, embracing them on the front steps. As though this is something he'd want the world to see.

I sit on the edge of the curb and stare at the house: this house in this nice neighborhood, which might have very well cost him a million dollars or more, that belongs to my father but does not belong to us.

It's my birthday. I'm seventeen today. There's no cake, no candles, no streamers, or songs. Just me, alone, on a curb, following the lies of a man whose life I once thought I understood.

I make my birthday wish anyway.

I sit and I wait. And then I close my eyes.

And I make a wish.

I make a wish that one day I'll understand.

I make a wish that one day I'll be able to see the truth of it all.

An hour later, part of my wish comes true.

I have to scramble to hide behind a parked car when I

see my father come out of the building. And behind him, a tall, stylish brunette with bangs and an elegant skirt. He holds the door open and then lifts a stroller down the steps. There's a little boy in the stroller, and the woman, Paige, presumably, is holding the hand of a little girl who follows him down the steps. My father reaches his hand out to Paige and pulls her close.

The kids both have red hair, curly and wild, like my father's.

Like mine.

This is it.

There they are.

They're a beautiful family, model-perfect. It's like they stepped out of a catalog. Paige is young and pretty, and the kids are well dressed, the boy in khakis and a Cubs hat, the girl in a purple paisley dress, her hair in pigtails. She's clutching a stuffed lion. It's just like the one he brought for Mila.

More than anything, I think.

You matter, I think.

And then I think, I could follow them to dinner or to the park or whatever place they're going to.

But I've seen enough.

From this one sight alone, I have my answer.

I know what it's like to have a beautiful mother, a beautiful sister, a father who brings home toys from his fancy business trips abroad and who holds his wife's hand lovingly.

I know exactly what it's like to be them.

This family I see before me is beautiful and perfect.

And it's also a lie. A cruel and terrible lie.

I could run up to them, make myself known, ruin their lives just as much as he's ruined ours. And then I could run home, tell my mother about everything.

I could take them all down, ruin them all.

But then I think about Mila, her birthday wish, how she wants us all to be together.

I let my father and his other family turn the corner, out of sight, and I head back toward Bennett Village.

Instead of walking back through the park, I take the long route home down Lincoln Avenue.

I look in windows.

I sit at bus stops.

I stare at people.

I try to understand.

It's all too much.

I don't know where to go, what to do next.

I could text my dad. Or not.

I could talk to my mom. Or not.

I could keep it all to myself and pretend I never saw anything.

Nothing makes sense. I can't figure it out.

There are too many choices but no right answer.

Habits of an Effective Test Taker #7

More often than not, answers that are longer and contain more detail are the correct ones. Shorter answers are created quickly and are often throwaways that can be easily eliminated.

I stay at Sammie's another three nights. I don't bother going downstairs to get clean clothes. I don't want to run into anyone accidentally, not my mother, certainly not my father, and not even Mila. I buy a new toothbrush and some underwear, and Sammie lets me borrow her clothes. I text my parents that I'll be at Sammie's for a few days.

My mother calls me and begs me to come home, but after a few uncomfortable conversations, she finally agrees to let me be. My father, on the other hand, texts back: *This behavior is unacceptable. Come back when you are ready to have a conversation like an adult.*

What a jerk.

I go to work, make my way through the day even though Sammie won't be able to get her shifts changed back to mine until next week, and then I walk around the city, alone, while Sammie and her mom look at apartments in Morton Grove.

At night, Sammie distracts me by telling me stories about the O'Briens and Professor Cox and Mrs. Woodley. I half-hear them. They seem silly and pointless, but I don't say anything to Sammie. I just let her talk.

When I finally return home Thursday after work, my mom's on her computer at the dining room table, as usual. My dad's back, and he's on the couch watching *Wild Kratts* with Mila. She's got her head against his shoulder and her pinkie in her mouth.

No one looks up to say hello to me.

In their world, everything is fine. I am the one who's acting strange. I am the one who is illogical, emotional, childish. I am the one who's threatening their perfect harmony for no good reason.

I head to my room and shut the door.

My mom calls out to me: "I did your laundry. Everything in the basket is clean. You just need to fold it."

I sit at my desk and open my computer. I haven't checked my e-mail in five days, not because I couldn't do it at Sammie's, but because I've been on a mission to avoid the world as much as possible. AP scores are scheduled to come this week, but I haven't checked, mainly because I haven't been able to face the results.

But now that I'm here, seeing my world as it is—the lies and disappointments that it's built upon—I figure, what's another layer of failure?

It's there. An e-mail from the College Board that my scores are ready, that I just need to log in to my account to see the results.

I take a deep breath.

Here we go.

AP English Language: 2 (Possibly qualified)

European History: 2 (Possibly qualified)

Physics B: 5 (Extremely qualified)

How is that even possible? Physics is my worst subject. How could I have aced the physics exam and bombed both English and history?

I print out two copies of the results. I grab my backpack and stuff it with clothes from the laundry basket. I close my computer, grab a different pair of shoes, fold one copy of my results and put it in my pocket.

I take the other copy to the dining room and throw it on the table.

"I suppose you'll want to have a talk about why I got screwed up on my AP tests."

My mom looks up at me. "What?"

"Vivi?" Mila jumps up from the couch. She runs to me and wraps her arms around my waist. "I didn't see you come in."

"Hi, Mila."

My father walks over to the table and picks up the paper.

"I didn't get perfect scores on my exams like you wanted. In fact, I pretty much bombed them."

"Where have you been?" Mila looks at my backpack. "Where are you going?"

"Nowhere." I kiss the top of her head. "Out."

He looks at the paper. "You got a five in physics. . . ."

"But I got twos on my other exams. And two B's on my report card. So yeah. There goes Stanford. They'll never accept me now."

My father looks up at me. "After that photo debacle, I'm surprised you thought they'd still even consider you at all."

"Wow," I say, shocked. "Real nice, Dad. Way to support me when I'm down. It's not enough that I messed up on my exams, you've got to remind me about how I messed up my personal life as well—"

My mom snatches the paper out of my father's hand and crumples it up. "It doesn't matter," she says. "I don't care about these stupid tests."

"But he does," I say.

Mila starts to cry. "What's going on? Why aren't you sleeping here?" She pulls at my backpack and then at my arm. "Stay, please. Daddy, can't you make her stay?"

"Yes," he says. "Of course I can make her stay. Viviana, you are not going anywhere, not while I'm home, not while you're living under my roof."

I laugh. "You know what, Dad? You're a liar."

I can't help it. I know I shouldn't say anything. At least not now. Not in front of Mila.

But I finally see him as he is. After all these years of

pushing me to be like him, now for him to just walk in here and pretend like the last six months never happened, like everything in his life isn't a lie. "You'll never be able to make me do anything again."

"Excuse me?" He steps toward me as though he wants to hit me.

"You heard what I said. You're a liar. And an ass."

"Viviana!" my mom yells. "Apologize to your father!"

"Vivi, why did you say that? Daddy's not an ass!"

"Mila!" My mom takes her by the shoulders, urges her down the hallway. "Go to your room! Now!"

But Mila resists. She pulls away from our mom and crawls underneath the dining room table and turns herself into a ball. She covers her ears and wails.

"I said NOW, Mila."

I'm sorry, Mila, but Daddy's a liar.

I'm sorry, Mila, but Daddy has another family.

I'm sorry, Mila, but he loves this other family more than anything.

More than us.

I get out of there as fast as I can, before it all comes out.

I run down the hall toward the emergency stairwell. I push the door open and run down the stairs.

I'm on the fourteenth floor when I hear an upstairs door slam.

"Viviana, wait!" It's my father.

I start jumping down the steps, two, three, five at a time. I need to get away from him.

I'm on the ninth floor when his voice bellows again through the corridor: "Viviana! Come back here! NOW!"

When I was younger, the sound of his voice would have scared me into submission. Even the me of six months ago would have stopped for him. The me of six months ago would have turned around, gone back upstairs, begged for forgiveness.

But right now, the sound of his voice pushes me to run faster, to jump farther, to leap down the steps.

His steps echo above me. He is racing to catch up.

I'm on the fourth floor.

I'm on the third floor.

I'm almost there.

I just need to get to the lobby and out the front door.

I won't come back.

I won't come back to Bennett Tower.

Not ever again.

I'll figure out somewhere else to stay.

I'll ask Sammie to call someone else for me.

Maybe Virgo. Or Evan.

I'll find any other way to live my life, so long as it's far away from my father and his sick, twisted life.

I'm on the second floor when I feel my feet slip on the steps.

Gravity pushes me down. I roll and I fall and I tumble. I land on my back, my body just another collapsed, failed product of Benjamin Lowe.

I gasp for oxygen. My lungs are empty of air—the hard impact has knocked them clean. I struggle to sit up, to move, to breathe, to stand up and keep my body moving, away from him. His steps are coming closer and closer. I need to go. I need to get away. But the sharp spasms stab my chest, and all I can do is crawl.

All I can do is grovel.

I look up. The corridor spins above me.

"Viviana?" He's caught me. "Are you okay?"

I can't do it.

I can't breathe.

I'm suffocating. I'm choking. I'm dissolving, melting, drowning because of him.

He's here now, his hand on my back, telling me to breathe, that I'm okay, that he's here for me, that I just need to suck in the air, to let my lungs relax, to tell them to settle.

For a brief moment, I let him tell me what to do. I let his words in. I let him convince my lungs that they need to relax. I let him tell my body that it needs to breathe.

The oxygen returns. My lungs become whole again. My body is in pain—my lungs, my head, my back—but I can move. I can sit up.

I can see him clearly.

My father, Benjamin Lowe, is a dangerous man. He is manipulative and strange and selfish and mean.

And then I hear his voice, loud and clear. "Viviana, what is this all about? You're acting crazy. You need to calm down."

That's it.

I can't do this anymore.

"Calm down? You want me to calm down? How can I? More than anything, Dad! More than anything!"

"What in God's name are you talking about?"

"Paige, Dad. And your other kids. You love her—you love them—more than anything."

My voice lifts into the corridor like thunder, like lightning, like the rage of a thousand storms.

"You love *them* more than anything."

He sits on the step next to me. "Oh hell."

"Yeah. Oh hell. I know *everything*, Dad. I followed you. I saw them. I saw how you kissed her and you hugged them. You got her a lion? A lion, Dad? You couldn't even be creative enough to get something different for your different children?"

I stand up. My body throbs with the pain of my collapse, but I somehow feel stronger than I ever have, maybe in my entire life.

"You want to have an adult conversation?" I ask. "Fine. Here it is: I'm done. You've lost me, for good. You have no right to judge me or push me or criticize me, ever again. You can't control me anymore."

I stumble down the steps, away from him.

"Wait—" He stands up and reaches out to me. "You're hurt."

"No!" I yell. "Don't you dare follow me. It's done. It's over. There's nothing you can do to help me now."

I end up back at Sammie's only because I know now that he'll leave me alone. I send him one last text: *Tell Mom to let me be. If either of you even tries to come upstairs, I'll tell her what I know, and then everything will be over for you.*

Sammie's mom is kind to me. She doesn't ask me any

questions, probably because she's talked to my mom. She just lets me move in with them. She lets me eat their food and use their shampoo and sleep on their couch.

Sammie requests her original shift back from Mr. Bautista, so at least I have her by my side again. "It pays to know people in low places," she jokes. I try to laugh, but it comes out hollow.

That's because I am hollow.

I am a sore, broken mess of a person.

Nothing can fix me.

PART FOUR

Viviana Rabinovich-Lowe's College Application Checklist

☐ ~~May: AP Exams~~ *bombed*

☐ ~~June–July: Design and Engineering Summer Academy~~ *thwarted*
☐ ~~July: Work on College Apps~~
☐ ~~August: Work on College Apps; Study for SAT~~

☐ ~~September: Finalize Stanford Application~~

Take
☐ ~~October: SAT General Test;~~
~~— Submit Early Action Application to Stanford~~ *Why bother?*

Professor Cox is back. It's been six weeks, seven thunder-storms, and five more Episodes since the tomato attack in June. Everyone's talking about the unusual summer weather: rain sixteen days this month, and it's the middle of August. On the very few hot days, the pool is packed with kids, and I want to scream from the chaos and the claustrophobia, and on the very many cool and rainy days, the pool is empty, and I want to scream from boredom.

Today is one of those days.

It hasn't rained since the morning, but the sky is gray and dark, and Professor Cox is the only one in the water. He's swimming in circles and singing kids' songs to him-self: "If You're Happy and You Know It," "She'll Be Coming 'Round the Mountain," "The Ants Go Marching." Virgo's on duty, and after a while, he joins in his deep baritone voice. Professor Cox gives him a thumbs-up and then sings more loudly.

"This is so depressing," Sammie says. "This is just the

summer of suck. It won't stop raining, you're a mess, in one month I'm moving to a new apartment and a new school, and I now have to listen to those two all afternoon."

"Not exactly summer perfection, huh?"

"Nope. Far from it." She reads from her phone. "'Your mood may be swayed by electronic disturbances from the planetary shifts that are inevitable and real. It's not too late to take charge, though. Change it up. Move a little. Play some music and dance. Take a risk, and you'll find that those around you will respond in kind. Perhaps even the planets will move with you, too.'"

"Is that mine or yours?"

"Mine." She presses a few more buttons on her phone. "You don't want to know yours. 'Worries about the integrity of important relationships in your life . . . taking action . . . letting them know what's on your mind—'"

"That's enough, thanks."

"Yeah. Like I said."

Evan arrives for work, and Sammie and I shift in our seats uncomfortably.

He comes into the office, stuffs his jacket into his locker, and puts on his whistle.

He looks at me. "Are you okay?"

"What?" It's the first time he's talked to me in a month.

"I don't know. You look like you're upset about something. Is everything okay?"

"Yeah, I mean, kind of." I look at Sammie. "I'm fine."

"Okay . . . ," he says, but he says it like it's a question, like he doesn't believe me. He has a guitar with him, which he places under the counter next to me. "Do you mind if I leave this here? Can you keep an eye on it?"

"Sure," I say. "Go for it."

Sammie perks up. "You should play for us. Professor Cox and Virgo are in the middle of a sing-along, and my horoscope is saying that I should get up and dance." She kicks my leg. "Vivi, wouldn't you like to hear him play?"

What is she doing? "Um, sure?"

Evan gives me a funny look. It's a look of betrayal. Of distrust. Like he knows that the girl who kissed him and then went crazy and threw him away is lying to him. Again.

"Maybe," he says. "We'll see." He grabs his rescue tube and heads toward the water.

"What was that?"

"I know you're in crisis mode, but I'm not giving up on you."

"You honestly think that getting into a relationship with someone is going to be the thing that helps me?"

"No," she says. "I think confronting your parents and demanding that they pay for the many years of therapy they owe you is going to be the thing that helps. But you have to face the truth, Vivi. Besides me, you don't have anyone else. And I'm leaving the city in a month. So having another friend, someone like Evan, who genuinely likes you, who genuinely cares about you, can't hurt, either."

"Ugh." I slide into my chair. "I really hate you sometimes, you know that?"

"Yeah, I know," she says. "Because you know I'm right. I'm always right."

The rains come again a few hours later, complete with a cold wind, lightning and thunder, and small chunks of hail. Professor Cox doesn't want to get out of the water, even though he's getting blasted by ice, and Virgo has to yell at him that the pool is closed and that if he doesn't get out, he'll have to call security. That doesn't work, either, but Professor Cox gets out when Evan finally yells, "Okay, then, Professor Cox, how about the police?"

He scrambles out of the water and runs out of the pool area, leaving his towel on a chair.

Evan and Virgo duck into the office out of the hail.

"I feel bad," Evan says. "I shouldn't have threatened him with the police."

Virgo asks, "Do you think he'll be teaching in the fall?"

"No," Sammie says. "He's going on a sort of emergency sabbatical for a year. My mom's been helping to advocate for him. But I don't know if she's going to help as much after we move."

"You're moving?" Virgo asks. "Where to?"

"The suburbs." Sammie sticks her finger in her mouth and fake gags.

"A new school for senior year?" Evan says. "That sucks."

"Well, maybe," Sammie says. "I'm thinking about getting my GED this fall and taking classes at the local community college in the spring."

This is news to me. "You're going to do what?"

"I've been talking to my mom about it. I don't want to start over twice—first at a new high school, and then again when I go to college next year. She's a little worried about me being by myself so much, but she also agrees that I'm old enough to decide for myself. She told me to take a few weeks to think about it. I mean, she hasn't even rented a new place yet. Our lease is up in September, so I have some time to figure it out."

I know Sammie is going through so much, like me—losing her dad last year, now moving out of the city—but I can't help feeling a little bit jealous that she's dealing with it all so well, that she's figuring things out.

"That sounds very cool," Virgo says. "I think you've got to do what's right for you."

Evan pulls out his guitar and strums a few chords. "Sometimes that's easier said than done."

The hail beats down harder now. The chunks are pretty substantial, the size of small pebbles. They crack and burst on the cement. Virgo shuts the office door. "This storm is crazy."

Evan plucks at his guitar. He plays a few scales and then starts to hum. He looks up at me and smiles.

"Play something for us," I say. "I want to hear you sing."

I can feel the surprise in the room, from Evan especially.

"Really?" he asks.

"Yes, really."

"What do you want me to play?"

"I don't know. Anything. Something you wrote?"

Evan leans into his guitar and begins with a soft song. It's so quiet, at first, that I can hardly hear it, what with the pounding of the hail above. But then his volume picks up and he begins to strum at a quick rhythm. He starts to sing.

His voice is smooth and clear. I recognize the subject of the song. I recognize the time and the place. I recognize the moment. "Follow me into the water," he sings, "away from the falling sky, where we'll dance, maybe kiss, maybe question the world. I'll swim into your arms. How quiet it will be."

He finishes the song, and Virgo and Sammie explode into applause.

"Evan," Sammie exclaims, "I had no idea! You're amazing!"

"I don't know about amazing," he says. "But thanks. That means a lot to me."

He looks up at me. "What'd you think?"

I want to cry. Here's this person, this nice, kind, gentle person. He likes me. He asks me how I am. He writes songs about me. Back in June, when we were having real conversations about parents and life and our desires for more, he was nice and funny and kind.

And yet. It's the wrong time. I can't return the feeling. I'm empty. I have nothing left inside to give.

"It was beautiful," I force myself to say. "Really beautiful."

It's the truth.

The hail lets up, and now it's only rain falling down on us. Virgo stands up. "Well, pool's closed, and we've got another free afternoon. We could head back up to the roof, have another game of Extreme Ping-Pong? If I remember correctly, Evan needs to redeem himself."

"Better yet," Evan says, "you guys want to come up to our place? Our dorm has a pool table. We could try for a game of Extreme Billiards—"

Sammie jumps up. "I love that idea!"

"I hate that idea," I say. "Extreme Billiards sounds extremely dangerous."

"Come on," Sammie says. "It's not like you have to be home—"

"I kind of just want to go to your apartment and take a nap."

"No," Sammie says, laughing. "No nap. You're coming with us. End of story."

"Ugh," I groan. "But I'm *so* tired."

Evan looks at me. "Come with us, Vivi. It'll be fun. You can help me beat Virgo with your Extreme tournament skills."

I think about what Sammie said. That she's going to be gone soon. That I'm going to need a friend besides her. Someone who cares about me. "Okay," I say. "Fine. I'll come up for a little bit." *But no kissing,* I think to myself.

No kissing, no boyfriends, no more breaking hearts.

We take the bus a few miles north to the campus of St. Mary's. Their dorm is an old brick building a few blocks away from the central quad. We enter the lobby, to find it packed with people. "Crap," Virgo says. "I forgot. It's Sleepover Weekend."

"What's that?"

"A bunch of incoming freshmen stay overnight so that they can get a preview of college life," Evan explains. "The RAs fill them with free pizza and get them drunk and then make them promise not to tell their parents. It's why we have the highest student satisfaction rate in Illinois, particularly among underclassmen."

We head to the basement, where the pool table is, but some of the weekend visitors are in the midst of a game. "Damn high schoolers," Virgo says, and then he looks at Sammie and me. "No offense."

"None taken," Sammie says.

Virgo and Evan give us a quick tour of the common area. It smells like microwave popcorn and patchouli (a sort of gross combination), but it also makes me want to live on my own.

I can't believe that I'm not going to Stanford. That I bombed everything except that stupid physics test. I know there are other options, other colleges that I could still get into, but I haven't even thought about any. My father was so hell-bent on my following in his footsteps, I never even thought to research anything else.

The thought of it makes me dizzy and a little nauseous, but the last thing I need is to have an Episode right now. I take a deep breath and try to calm myself down.

Evan and Virgo lead us up to their room on the fifth floor. Virgo unlocks the door and pushes it open. "Welcome to our man cave."

"It's way cleaner than I expected," Sammie says. And it is. The decor is sort of typical boy—navy blue and gray comforters, a few posters on the walls, and Christmas lights strung on their bunk beds—but overall, it's pretty nice, and it smells much better than the common room.

"I'll take that as a compliment." Virgo plugs in his phone and turns on Spotify. "Tame Impala?"

"That works." Evan sits down on the bottom bunk—his bed, I presume—while Virgo climbs to the top. Sammie takes the one chair in the room, so that the only place for me is either next to Evan on the bed or on the floor. I choose the floor.

Virgo leans over the top bunk. "Want to contribute to the satisfaction rate?"

"Are you seriously thinking about getting us drunk?" Sammie says. "Thanks, but no thanks."

"No, you dork." Virgo laughs. He sits up and pulls out his phone. "I'm hungry and I was just going to offer all the free pizza you want."

"Oh, got it," Sammie says. "Sure. That sounds good."

After a few minutes of debating crust thickness and toppings (we settle on corn bread, half–Canadian bacon and pineapple, half-pepperoni), Virgo tries to call in our order. "An hour and a half for delivery versus half an hour pickup? Forget that. I'll just come get it."

Evan takes a few cans of pop out of the small fridge next to the desk and passes them around to us. We toast: "To rainy August days, drunk freshmen, and pizza deliberation."

Evan takes out his guitar and starts to play again. I lean against the bed and watch him. I can't help but feel sad at the thought of him—the thought that there's this really nice person who I can't let into my life—not because of who he is, but because of how hurt I am.

My phone dings and I pull it out of my bag. Sammie's sent me a covert text: *You are smitten.*

I don't write back. Instead, I just glare at her and shake my head.

About twenty minutes later, Virgo jumps down from the top bunk. "Time to get the 'za."

"I'll come with you!" Sammie says before she turns and winks at me.

They are out the door before I can protest or offer to join them or figure out some excuse for not being left alone here with Evan.

Thankfully, they leave the door wide open. The hallway is packed with the laughter and running of all the weekend visitors, but in here it's dark, and it's relatively quiet. It's just Evan and me, and I'm not sure what to say or do.

Evan puts away his guitar and then he sits on the floor next to me. "May I?"

I nod. He's so close, I can feel his warmth, hear his breath, smell his clothes—a perfect mixture of fresh dampness from the rain and fabric softener. He's familiar and comfortable, and yet I feel like I should maybe get up and run far away from him.

But I don't.

He looks at me. "How are you?"

I laugh. "You're always asking me that."

"Am I?" He smiles. "Well, I guess it's because I want to know."

"I'm okay, I guess."

"That's not very convincing."

"It's been a rough summer," I say. "A very rough summer."

He hangs his arms over his bent knees and nods. "Seems like it. Want to talk about it?"

"Not particularly," I say. "But thank you."

I don't feel like telling him, but I do feel this strange desire, this need to lean against him, to rest my head on his shoulder.

So I do.

He leans back against me, and then he kisses the top of my head.

"You're so nice to me."

"I try."

"I do remember," I say finally. "Anne Boyd's party. Seven Minutes in Heaven."

"You remember?"

"The last fifteen seconds? You were my first kiss. Of course I remember."

He laughs. "Oh no! I was your first kiss? I kind of want to apologize or something. I hope I didn't ruin you for life."

"No way." I shake my head. "Not at all. If anything, you set the bar high. And, I mean, nothing's hotter than making out on the uncomfortable edge of a cold bathtub. Nothing has compared since."

He laughs. "Seriously. What could be better than shower curtains and shaving cream?"

"Wait a minute. So I wasn't your first kiss? You were what, twelve?"

"Thirteen, thank you very much. And I'll admit: I'd played Seven Minutes in Heaven before. In fact, I was drafted into the minor leagues at the end of eighth grade."

We both crack up.

"In all honesty," he says, "you were my second kiss."

"Really?"

He nods.

"And you set the bar high, as well."

All of this talk about kissing really makes me want to kiss him.

I think we're about to, when a group of kids runs down the hallway screaming, which startles us both.

"You'd think they'd never been away from home before," Evan says with a laugh, which breaks the weird intensity of the moment.

"They probably haven't," I say. "I mean, my parents rarely let me go anywhere, so I kind of get it."

He looks at me. "They're pretty protective, huh?"

"Well, they were. Now they don't know what to do with me."

Now there's not much they can do with me, I think.

"Viviana—"

I look up.

"Vivana, is that you?"

"Oh no." Standing at the edge of the open door is Dean. Dean of the HushDuo legacy. Dean of the Biggest Ass on the North Side of Chicago legacy. Dean—the guy who ruined my reputation and broke my heart.

Evan looks at me. "You two know each other?"

"I'm Dean." He steps inside the room and puts out his hand. He's holding a red cup that smells like some kind of hard liquor and his eyes are glazed over. He's plastered. "I knew Viviana in a past life." He says this with a creepy, drunk smirk on his face. My heart drops to the pit of my core. "We used to go to school together, before I transferred out of that hellhole of a place."

"Um . . . okay," Evan says before releasing Dean's hand.

Dean looks at me. "Are you applying to St. Mary's?"

I stumble over my words. "No—I mean, I'm not sure—I mean—"

"I never took you as a local girl. I thought you had bigger and better dreams, like Stanford or Harvard or some snotty place like that."

What an ass. Which is what I want to say. But I'm too shocked or hurt or confused by the fact that he's standing five feet in front of me to articulate anything of value. Plus, the last thing I need is to explain all that to Evan.

My phone dings. It's a text from Sammie: *If you haven't started sucking his face, make it happen now, because we are on our way back.*

I ignore her message and throw my phone back into my bag.

Dean's still standing there, staring at me. "After everything that happened, I'm shocked, and frankly somewhat appalled, that you still have a phone. That you're still willing to take that risk again."

Oh no.

No, no, no.

I look at Dean, and then Evan, and I think about everything else that Dean could say right now that could ruin this—whatever this is—between Evan and me.

"It's—it's just a phone— I mean, how dare you even stand there—" I try to get the words out, to stand up for myself, but I am immediately nauseous and dizzy—and my breath is gone—completely gone. I am sitting firmly on the floor, but I feel like I'm falling, spiraling, plunging back into the disaster that is my past.

Evan gets up and starts to close the door as a signal for

Dean to leave. "You're clearly bothering her, and so I think it's time for you to go."

Dean chugs the rest of his drink. "And I think it's none of your business."

"You're standing in my room and clearly bothering my friend, so it very well is my business."

"You mean your *girlfriend*?" Dean asks with a laugh. He sounds like a six-year-old.

I really want to throw up.

"And *that's* none of *your* business," Evan says. He gestures toward the door. "I'm going to ask you one more time to leave."

For some reason, Dean's refusing to budge.

I catch my breath. "Dean, would you just go? Please?"

"Does your friend here—" He's laughing and slurring his words. "Does he know about your texting habits?"

"Dean, please stop—"

"Does he know how you like to break up with people over text? How you don't even allow them the courtesy of a face-to-face conversation? How you like to—"

Oh God, my heart.

"You can stop." Evan puts his hand on Dean's shoulder. "Now."

Dean laughs and then tries to sucker punch Evan, but thankfully Evan's too fast and Dean's too weak and too drunk to make the hit.

Instead of punching his face, Dean sort of lands weakly into Evan's chest, which allows Evan to grab hold of him by the shoulders and basically push him out the door. "You're letting hot air in the room. Be safe now." And he slams the door in Dean's face.

"Ex-boyfriend?" Evan says.

"Something like that." I nod, stunned, unable to say anything else.

"I should call campus security."

"Please don't."

Evan nods. Thankfully, he doesn't pry further. Instead, he just turns up the music and sits next to me, his shoulder pressed against mine.

I do my best to catch my breath. I try to make my breathing slow and quiet. Somehow, it works.

A few minutes later, Virgo and Sammie return with pizza in hand.

Evan doesn't say anything to them about Dean or what just happened. We spend the rest of the night in their room, eating pizza and listening to music. The three of them talk about everything from school to Kanye West to *Game of Thrones* to the Mars One project and whether or not they would apply. I mostly just listen.

Evan doesn't ask me how I am anymore, but it's okay.

I feel really good, sitting here with him next to me.

He doesn't have to ask.

**Mistakes to Avoid Your
Senior Year of High School #1**

**You should challenge yourself in new ways, but
don't overextend yourself, either. It's not worth
taking all AP classes if it lands you a C or you
can't pass the exam.**

Every Monday morning, I sneak back into my apartment
when I know that no one will be home. I usually text my
dad to tell him to make sure the apartment is empty so I
can go in by myself, and he always texts back a simple *Okay*.
I woke up on Saturday morning back in Sammie's bed and
found a multisentence text from him saying that he was
leaving for Singapore for a week, and that the apartment
would be clear for me today. He also wrote that I should

come back home now that he's gone, that my mother and Mila need me and miss me.

But I'm not ready to move back in. I'm afraid that I might end up telling them everything I know. I don't want to be the one to ruin their lives.

I unlock the front door.

The apartment smells like onion and garlic. I miss my mom's cooking so much. I miss her.

But I just can't face her yet.

I head to my room. She's made my bed and straightened up my desk and left a basket of clean, folded clothes on my bed. There's a drawing there, too, from Mila, with my paycheck from Bennett Tower, Inc., and a note from my mom: *Come back when you're ready. I love you, Viviana. I love you unconditionally.*

I fold the papers and stuff them in my backpack.

I walk down the hallway to Mila's room, which is a mess, as usual. The floor is covered with stuffed animals, Legos, uncapped markers, and crumpled clothes. My parents never let me live like this when I was her age. My dad would yell at me if I even left my bed unmade. I don't feel jealous so much as relieved that Mila is experiencing a freedom they never gave me. It actually makes me hopeful in some way.

I go into my parents' room. The bed is made, and everything is clean, as my mom likes it. The photos on the walls are perfectly lined up. She had my dad put them up the week after she was diagnosed with the cancer. She knew she was going to have to rest in bed for months, and she said she didn't want to stare at blank walls, that she wanted to stare at the people she loved more than anything else.

There are photos of me as a child with my mom's family in Israel on various trips that I hardly remember taking before Mila was born, and then there are photos of all of us together at the hospital when Mila was born, at her first day of kindergarten, of my eighth-grade graduation.

My mom's put a few more photos on her dresser, ones that I haven't seen before. They're from my old Instagram account, photos of Sammie and me, our silly faces filling up the frames. She must have printed them out before I canceled my account. I never knew she'd done this.

I pick up one of the pictures. We took it freshman year, long before Sammie's dad died, before my mom got sick. It's been over two years since then. We look younger, of course—Sammie still has braces, and I'm sporting my sorry attempt at bangs—but even more, we look different because we look happy. We were happy. We were different people completely. Maybe Professor Cox was right. We didn't really know anything about the world. Maybe we still don't. Maybe it will only get worse, like he said.

I place the picture back on the dresser. My dad has left some of his stuff here in his wooden tray—a broken watch, a pair of sunglasses, a pile of receipts. I leaf through the receipts. There's nothing too exciting—some from airport cafés and taxis in Singapore, all with the word *work* written on top, and then more from home: Starbucks, Macy's, Target.

I start going through his drawers, looking for something. I don't know what exactly. Pictures of them, maybe. Letters. Something, anything, to explain who they are, why they're in his life, why he's decided to create one in theirs.

I pull out his shirts, his pants, his socks, everything. There's nothing here, but I empty the drawers anyway. I clean them out. I throw it all on the floor.

The last drawer is nearly empty when I hear something heavy fall out. I drop to the ground. I scramble through the fabric and find it: a set of keys with a label attached. The bastard was dumb enough to leave them here, and even dumber to label them: *Geneva Terrace*.

My legs start to shake, and then my heart quickly follows.

They're the keys to the other house. He's left them here, hidden in his clothes, and now I've found them—they're in my hand.

There's a rustling at the front door, a turn of the lock, and voices—my mom's voice, and Mila's—she's crying. What the hell. It's ten-thirty, and they're not supposed to be back until this afternoon.

I slide the keys into my pocket and quickly stuff all of my dad's clothes into his drawers, careful not to slam them closed. I slip out of their room and tiptoe down the hallway toward the living room, the keys burning in my pocket.

"Viviana!" Mila screams as she runs to me. "Are you back? Are you home for good?"

"No, I'm not." I look up at my mom. "What's going on? Why are you guys home so early?"

"I threw up!" Mila says, with a proud smile on her face. "We were on a field trip to the Field Museum and I got carsick on the bus and I threw up all over Nicholas Smith. He had to go home, too."

"Are you okay now?"

"She's fine," my mom says. "But, Viviana, thank God you're here. Could you stay home with her for a few hours? I'm missing my class."

"Mama, I have to be at work at one."

"*Please,* Viviana. I will be back in two hours. I have a meeting with my professor at eleven. I was going to cancel, but he wants to talk to me about an internship—a paid one—and it would mean the world to me if you could stay so I could go."

"I really don't think I should—"

Mila pulls at my arm and gives me a sharp, angry look. "Why don't you want to stay with me? Are you mad at me, too?"

I look at my mom. "What if she throws up again?"

My mom goes into the kitchen and pulls out Gatorade, emergency saltines, and applesauce from the cabinets. "She won't, but just in case, only feed her this." And then before I can say anything else, my mom grabs her briefcase, kisses Mila on the forehead, and runs out the door.

"Why won't you tell me?"

It's the twentieth time she's asked me in the last hour, and for the twentieth time, I respond by saying, "Because it's none of your business."

We're curled up on the couch watching *Planet Earth* on Netflix, and I'm trying to get her just to watch the show, to get her to stop asking me so many questions, especially since all I can think about are these keys in my pocket.

"Is it because of Daddy?"

I ignore her question and keep my focus on the TV. "Why is it called a flying lemur if it doesn't fly and it's not a lemur?"

She stares at me. "It's called a colugo. It lives in Borneo. And it's not flying. It's gliding." And then: "Is it because of their almost divorce?"

"This is crazy!" I ignore her question and point to the screen. "Look at how far they travel through the air. How do they do that?"

"It's the same as a flying squirrel. It's not that exciting." And then: "Is it because you're mad that they won't pay for your Academy camp thing?"

"But how does it do that? It moves like a Frisbee."

"Is it because of what happened at school with your ex-boyfriend and the picture you sent him?"

I nearly fall off the couch. "What? How do you know about—"

"I live in this house, too," she says. "The walls are thin, and I have really good hearing."

"But that's none of your business!"

"Why won't any of you tell me anything?"

"Because," I say, "you're too young to understand."

"I am NOT too young! I'm not stupid. I see everything. I know that Mama and Daddy are having problems. And I know that you're having problems and they're so bad that you have to move out, and now Daddy's gone and Mama's busy with school and—and—" She starts to cry. "No one cares about me anymore and no one will tell me anything!"

She collapses into the couch and screams into the cushions.

"Oh, Mila, no. That's not true. That's the opposite of true. I care about you. I care about you so much."

"Then why won't you come home?" Her voice is muffled from the pillows. I sit down next to her and put my hand on her back.

"Don't rub my back. Answer my question. Why aren't you home?"

"I just— I can't be here right now."

"Are you going to come home soon?"

"If you take your face out from the couch, then yes, maybe, soon."

She lifts her head. "Really?"

"Yes, really." I'm not sure I mean it, but I want her to calm down. "I love you, Mila."

"Okay," she says, crossing her arms across her chest. "I'm glad you love me."

"We all do." *More than anything,* I think.

She doesn't say anything to that. Instead, she makes me sit down next to her, and then she puts her pinkie in her mouth and rests her head on my shoulder. We sit like that, watching TV in silence, my fingers gripping the keys in my pocket, not knowing what to do next.

**Mistakes to Avoid Your
Senior Year of High School #2**

**Senior year is actually too late to start thinking
about college, especially for the top schools.
Start preparing for the process of applying to
colleges in your junior year, making sure to be
involved and engaged in all aspects of your
educational career.**

The storms return the next day. The forecasters are predicting an "Extreme Summer Storm," complete with more hail, high humidity, and damaging winds. The suburbs may even see tornadoes. It's a "supercell" of a storm that's certain to damage property. Mr. Bautista orders Virgo to close the pool and we all get text messages not to report for work until Thursday.

Sammie and I get the text while we're getting ready.

"Hallelujah," Sammie says, throwing her brush in the drawer.

"No work for two days. I mean, it sucks we're stuck here and can't go to the beach or something, but at least we get a few days off."

"Yeah, I guess."

"You guess?"

"I'm not so good at doing nothing," I say. "I thought I wanted inertia, but I'm not so good at it. Plus, being at work—even when the helicopter moms are complaining about the no-floatie rule—it distracts me, you know?"

"Yeah. I get it," she says. "Well, we have the whole day. What do you want to do?"

"I don't know. Nothing?"

We both laugh at first, but then she gets quiet. "Vivi, you've seemed more upset these past few days. Did you hear from your dad? Did something else happen?"

"What? No." I haven't told Sammie about finding the keys or seeing Mila or the fact that she knows about the photo. Just thinking about it makes my heart race. The last thing I need is to talk about it, too. "I'm just tired, I guess."

Our phones buzz. *Extreme Summer Storm calls for game of Extreme Summer Ping-Pong Championship, wouldn't you say?* It's a text from Virgo to Evan, Sammie, and me.

"Awesome," Sammie says. "Want to?"

I nod.

She looks up at me. "They'll be here in about forty minutes. Want me to give you a crown braid?"

I shrug. "Sure. Thanks. I can do whatever you want, too."

"Okay, turn around." She starts combing my hair into strands. "We've got to make you look good for Evan."

"Sammie, come on. Stop. That's not happening. I will not destroy my friendship with you over a guy."

"He's *not*. Anyway, I'm not into guys who are totally into my BFF."

I smile. "Okay. Fine. Stop, though, please. After that whole thing with Dean, I doubt anything's going to happen as it is."

"Fine." She tugs my hair into a braid. "I will. Whatever you say."

I have to admit: Playing Extreme Ping-Pong during an Extreme Summer Storm on the thirty-eighth floor of a building is a much better distraction than sitting at work all day. Evan's also brought his guitar, and Virgo's brought a violin, and in between matches, they play songs for us while the building shudders from the wind and thunder.

We spend the morning going back and forth between Ping-Pong, songs, and sitting on the floor and watching the passing storms. Then, around twelve-thirty, we go back down to Sammie's to gather leftovers for lunch.

"My mom made dinner last night. Do you guys like Filipino food?"

"I'll eat anything," Evan says.

"Even chicken innards and pork bits?"

"Yes, probably," he says.

Virgo raises his hands. "Thanks, but I'll pass on both."

"I'm just kidding." Sammie takes the food out of the

fridge. "Today's menu is just chicken macaroni salad and pork adobo, no innards or bits included."

She leans into the fridge and pulls out a six-pack of Coke. We help her grab plates, napkins, and utensils, then head back upstairs. She spreads a picnic blanket on the ground near the window, and we fill ourselves on her mom's awesome food.

"Your mom's adobo is the best," I say. "I am so going to miss it."

"It's not like we're moving to Canada. We'll still see each other on weekends."

"I know."

"What are you going to do after Sammie moves?" Virgo asks. "Are you going back home?"

"I guess. I mean, I have nowhere else to go." I take a sip of Coke. "Can we talk about something else? This conversation is depressing the hell out of me."

"Sure," Virgo says. "I'm sorry."

"No, it's fine. I'm just sick of talking about my problems. I want to hear about someone else's problems."

"I've got one," Evan says. He puts down his plate and then shifts uncomfortably. "I got a message from my ex-girlfriend last night."

"Whoa," Virgo says. "Joanna? The high school sweetheart?"

"You mean the tenth-grade sweetheart? The one I pledged my life to when I was fifteen, the one I thought I'd marry and grow old with? Yeah, that one."

"You seriously thought you were going to marry her?"

Virgo laughs. "No one should be talking about marriage when they're in high school."

"Well, we did." Evan's shoulders slump. "And then she broke my heart."

"How?" Sammie asks.

"She cheated on me. Even though we were going to different colleges, we promised to stay together, since we're only a few miles away. But then she got together with another guy her first week at Northwestern, and she told me about it a week later. Said she was racked with guilt and couldn't take it anymore."

"When you say 'got together,'" I ask, "you mean—"

"Well, almost got together," Evan says. "They didn't have sex. But they made out. And they got close."

"Dude," Virgo says. "You don't tell!"

I look at Virgo. "What do you mean, 'You don't tell'?"

"I mean, you don't tell." He pauses to take a drink. "Even if it's flirting with someone else. You keep that stuff to yourself."

"But then you're lying to your significant other," I say. "And your whole relationship is a farce!"

Virgo raises his hands. "Sorry. I didn't mean to get you so upset."

"I'm not upset," I say, lowering my voice. "I'm just—I just disagree."

"Wait," Evan says. "So let me ask you this. She called me last week and said she wants to try again, that she feels terrible about what she did. She wants me to forgive her and give her another chance."

I'm surprised he's telling me this, especially after our night in his dorm room.

"You could give her a chance—" Virgo starts to say.

"Nope," I say, interrupting him. "There are no more chances."

"So you don't give her credit for being honest?"

"Hell no."

"I agree with Viviana," Sammie says.

"Okay, let me ask you this," Virgo says. "Would it have been better if she'd kissed the guy and then lied about it to Evan?"

"No! She shouldn't have done it at all!" I say. "Why? Do you actually think she should have lied?"

"Hell yes," Virgo says. "What's it going to fix? She was never going to see that other guy again. It's like what she did with him happened in another dimension. It doesn't count."

"I'd rather know," I say.

"Are you sure about that?" Virgo says. "Are you really sure you'd rather know?"

I think about everything I *do* know—I feel for the keys that are burning a hole in my pocket.

I look at Virgo. And I pull out the keys. "Yes," I say. "Because I already do."

"What are those?" Sammie asks.

"I found these in my father's drawer. They're the keys to his other house."

"Oh, no," Sammie says.

Virgo picks up the keys. "What are you talking about?"

"What do you mean, 'his other house'?" Evan leans over

and takes them from Virgo's hands. He reads the label. "What's Geneva Terrace?"

Maybe it's the fact that they're all staring at me or maybe it's the thundering sky or maybe it's what Sammie said about how I need more people in my life who care about me. Or maybe it's the fact that Evan's being totally, completely honest with me and I actually do care about him, and so I want to do everything in my power to save him from another broken heart.

So I tell them.

About my father.

His other family. His two kids. His two lives.

I tell them everything.

"That's insane," Virgo says.

But Evan says nothing. He just hands me back the keys with a strange look, and I'm not sure if the expression on his face is one of pity or confusion or sudden and complete understanding about why I often act like a complete freak.

"I looked her up on Facebook," I continue. "She's in Acapulco on vacation, she and her kids—I mean their kids. She doesn't have any pictures of him, but a hundred bucks my dad's there, too. He said he's back in Singapore on work, but he's a compulsive liar, so . . ."

"She took his name?" Virgo says.

"Hyphenated. Paige Griffin-Lowe."

"That's bizarre. Do you think she knows about you?"

"I have no idea," I say. "But I'm thinking about going in."

"Into his house?" Sammie asks. "You're going to break in?"

"Is it really *his* house? Or is it technically mine? I mean, if I'm his daughter, then everything that belongs to him belongs to me, right?"

"I think you have a right to go in," Virgo says, holding his Coke up in a mock toast. "See what this family's story is."

"No," Sammie says. "She doesn't! Vivi, I get that you're upset, but this isn't going to help."

"It might help me understand—" I start to say.

"No!" Sammie snaps. "The only thing that will help is talking to him. And your mom. You have to confront this directly, not sneak into his house looking for answers that you know are not there."

"Sammie, why aren't you supporting me in this?"

"Because it's a dumb idea."

"Gee, thanks."

"I don't know why you always have to do this."

"Do what?"

"You make everything more complicated than it needs to be."

"Excuse me?"

"Forget it," Sammie says. "I shouldn't say anything."

"No," I say. "Go for it. You're obviously busting to say something, so say it."

"Okay, fine. You want to know? You make these impulsive choices, you don't think things through, and then you come to me and—"

"And then I come to you and you're sick of me? You're sick of my drama?"

"That's not what I was going to say."

"Then what, exactly, were you going to say?"

"You need to think it through. You need to face your problems directly, for once."

"Instead of you doing it for me."

Sammie bites her lip.

"You know what? I have thought this through. It's all I can think about." How dare she call me impulsive or dramatic. She's the one who's dedicated her life to the performing arts. "I'm going to act on those thoughts—and it's going to be quite deliberate."

I stand up.

"You're going there now?"

"Yes, Sammie, I'm going there now."

"But it's pounding rain out there."

"Are you coming with? Are you going to be a friend to me? I need a friend right now. Or are you going to continue to throw insults at me?"

"You need help, Vivi."

"You telling me that I need help isn't helping, Sammie. It never helps. It just makes me feel worse."

I grab my jacket and my bag, and I run out the door before she can find more ways to remind me that I'm losing my mind.

"Viviana, wait!"

It's Evan. I tap the button for the elevator again, even though I know it won't make it come faster.

"What do you want?"

"I'm coming with you."

"What?"

"Like you said, you need a friend right now."

I'm about to tell him to stay here, that he doesn't need my brand of crazy in his life, but then he puts his hand on my shoulder and says, "Let me in, Viviana. Will you let me be your friend?"

The elevator bell rings and the door opens.

"Okay," I say finally. "I will."

**Mistakes to Avoid Your
Senior Year of High School #3**

**Don't forget to ask your parents for help!
Parents can have experience and be a great
resource. Don't shy away from asking them to
support you in all your endeavors!**

The house is nice. Incredibly nice. Modern and new, with dark hardwood floors, bone gray walls, bookshelves that span the length of the room and hover over an old brick fireplace that's been painted white. There's hardly any evidence that kids live here—a white canvas fort with patterned blue-and-green pennant flags and some square baskets hiding toys in the corner of the living room. Granted, they're on vacation, but other than that fact, there's no kids' art on the walls, no pictures of them, nothing—there's just not much proof that an actual family lives here.

Evan and I head up the narrow stairwell to the second floor, where each kid has a bedroom—the girl's painted lavender and white, the boy's painted a deep shamrock green—and each is clean and tidy, just like the first floor. There's a third room, one that's bright turquoise, with white furniture—it's mostly modern, but there are a few stuffed animals on the bed. "I thought they had only two kids," he says.

"I thought so, too."

I step into the room and I know instantly that it belongs to a girl. A teenage girl. Someone about my age. The clues are obvious: a black-and-white pillow on the bed that says *Believe in Yourself;* block letters of the word L-O-V-E and then her name, E-L-L-A, hanging on the walls next to a Stanford pennant. This room has the most photos. They're collaged on the wall in the shape of a heart. I scan the photos and see her—his other daughter. She's older than I am—there are pictures of her in her high school graduation cap, one where she's holding her brother when he was a baby, and other photos of her standing with my dad—our dad—she's wearing a Stanford shirt, pointing to it with one hand and flashing a peace sign with the other. He's beaming with this huge, proud smile. The smile that I haven't seen from him in months.

We find the stairway to the third floor, which leads to Paige's bedroom suite. Including the bathroom and a huge walk-in closet and adjoining seating area with vaulted ceilings, the upstairs room is the length of the house, and about the size of our entire apartment at Bennett Village.

I sit down on a wooden bench at the foot of their king-size bed.

"You okay?"

"Yes." I take a deep breath and a laugh escapes my chest. "No. Did you ever have the wind knocked out of you?"

"Yeah. I fell ice-skating when I was ten. It hurt like hell."

"Happened to me a couple of weeks ago. I fell down some stairs. I thought *that* was my low point."

Evan sits down next to me.

"He's been holding out on us. He said I couldn't go to this summer program because he couldn't afford it. But he could have. This place shows me that he very easily could have." I think about Ella's room. "Or maybe he couldn't because he has to pay for Stanford."

Evan nods. "What do you think you'll do now?"

"Tell my mom?" It comes out as a question, not a statement, but the minute I say it, I know it's what I have to do. "She needs to know, right?"

"Maybe she already does?"

I look at him. The truth of what he just said hits me hard. "I hadn't thought of that. I bet you're right. I bet she knows already." I drop my head in my hands. "What is my life? I don't know how to deal with any of this."

"I think you're actually dealing with all this really well."

"What?" I laugh. "No. I don't think so."

"I don't see you running into any swimming pools with all your clothes on."

I consider his point. I'm not dizzy. I'm not hyperventilating. I'm not falling into an Episode. I'm in shock—yes—

but I also somehow feel an odd sense of calm. Like now that I have answers, at least I understand my life with a bit more clarity. I lift my head and look at him. I lean into his shoulder, and he wraps his arm around me. "Thank you for being my friend today."

"Of course," he says. "And plus, you've helped me."

"How's that?"

"Well, you've convinced me not to get back together with my ex."

"Ha." I look up at him. "Glad I could be of service."

He smiles at me. "It's the right decision. I'm really into this other girl anyway."

I smile back. "She sounds like a keeper."

"You're going to be okay. You know that, right?"

And just like that night in seventh grade, and that day under the umbrella, I lean in. And I kiss him.

He returns this kiss. It's soft and careful. The tension in my body releases at the touch of his lips on mine.

But then he pulls back. "No. Not again. Not like this."

"I'm so sorry." I stand up. "Sammie's right. I do make everything complicated."

"It's not that—it's just—this isn't the right place or the right time—"

"You're right." I want to love someone like you, I think. I want to trust someone like you. Someone honest and kind and nice. But I'm in my father's other house. "My life is a mess, and I'm broken, and you deserve someone who's not."

He tries to explain himself, but I tell him I don't want to talk about it anymore, I just want to leave.

He makes it worse by listening to my request and not

saying anything else and thus proving, once again, what a good friend he could have been if only I hadn't messed it up by kissing him again.

I can't go to Sammie's, I can't talk to Evan, and the last place I want to be is home with my mom and Mila, but unless I want to be homeless on the street, it's the only place I have.

I throw my dad's keys to Geneva Terrace in a garbage can on Clark Street, and then I make my way back through the rain to Bennett Tower, back to my real life, which is nothing but a lie.

By the time I get home, I'm soaked.

My mom and Mila are home. They're both at the dining room table, but oddly enough, my mom's not at her computer, and Mila's not sitting in front of the TV. They're in the middle of a Jenga game. Mila looks over the wobbly tower and smiles when she sees me. "I'm winning."

"There are no winners in Jenga," my mom says with a laugh. And then she looks at me. "Get yourself in the shower and come play with us."

"That's it?" I say. "No probing questions about where I've been or judgmental comments about how my aimlessness is bad for Mila?"

"We miss you, Viviana," my mom says. "I hope this time you're here to stay."

I go to the bathroom and strip down. I turn the water as hot as it can go. I sit on the floor of the tub and let the shower pound down on my back. My skin turns red under the heat of the water, but it's not enough to dissolve the pain. I'm home, and they are out there waiting for me to return to them dry and renewed, as though everything in our lives is normal and fine.

But I know it's not.

It'll never be normal or fine, ever again.

**Mistakes to Avoid Your
Senior Year of High School #4**

**Many students lose steam during the summer
between their junior and senior years. Of course,
some loss of motivation is inevitable. Now is not
the time to relax! Now is the time to think about
your future!**

I'm woken up an hour later by the sounds of notifications
from my phone. It's the hollow, quick ding of the text message bell, five in a row.

I roll over and reach into my bag. I don't know who could
be texting me so much.

I click through. They're all from Sammie:

OMG, Vivi, call me.

Evan saw the photo.

Someone at St. Mary's found the photo and showed Evan.
Virgo messaged me to see if it was really you.
I'm so sorry, Vivi. Call me. I'm here.
Oh God. The photo. *My* photo.
I scream into my pillow.
My mom and Mila come running into my room.
"Viviana, what's going on?"
"I can't— I can't— I can't—"
"Viviana, take a deep breath."
"I can't— I can't— I can't—"
"You're okay. I've got you."
"No. Mama. I can't—"
"You're home now. You're fine."
She's blurry, Mila's blurry; everything is a spinning, blurry mess.

Mila's glued against my wall, a look of pure terror in her eyes, and I want to calm down for her. I want to be in control for her. I want to be myself for her.

I let myself fall into my mom's arms. She whispers to me that she's sorry she's been so hard on me, she's sorry for everything she's done, and I'm not sure exactly what she means, but hearing her words, hearing her admit her own mistakes, feeling her arms around my shaking body—it makes me catch my breath and I collapse into her. I let her hold me up.

"Okay, what's going on?"

Normally when my mom says that Mila needs to give us time so we can have an "adult conversation," my sister whines and complains, but this time, she's allowed my mom to usher her into the living room without issue. Except for that one time in the hospital, Mila hasn't seen me in the middle of a full-blown Episode. I guess this one was enough to scare her away.

My mom presses an ice pack onto my forehead. "Come on, Viviana."

My heart's still racing from the Episode, and it gets worse when I think about asking my mom for the truth.

"Talk to me. I'm your mother."

I sit up and take a deep breath. "Do you know someone named Paige Griffin?"

My mom lets go of the ice pack and it drops on my chest.

"Oh no."

I sink back down into my bed. "So you know?"

She drops her head and nods.

"For how long?"

She motions for me to move over in my bed, and then she sits next to me, pulls the blanket over her chest. "A few years only. But—" Her voice drops to a whisper. "Yes, I've known for a while."

"How did you— Why did you stay with him?"

"You have to understand," she says. "I've only kissed one other human being. I've only been with one other human being. I've only loved one other human being: him. I've been honest and pure with my love for him."

"Ella was already born when you got together with him?"

She motions to Mila on the other side of the wall and shushes me to speak more quietly before she answers. "You mean when I fell in love with him? Yes. He was a graduate student and married and already had a child. But Ella does not belong to Paige. She is from his first arrangement.

"But I didn't know that. I didn't know anything about Ella or his other life. I knew that my parents had left for Israel and I was alone and in love with a man who promised to take care of me for the rest of my life. And he did. Your father did that for me."

"So you've stayed with him because of me? Because of Mila?"

My mom smiles softly. "No. I've stayed with him because I loved him." She wipes away tears from the corners of her eyes. "And, well, because right after I found out—first about Ella, then about this third woman, Paige—I followed them to the playground—" She's struggling to get out the words. "I saw her, kissing him, and his babies, younger than Mila—and then I got so sick—"

"Oh, Mama. I didn't realize—" I'm crying now, choking on my tears.

She looks up at me and smiles again, wipes the tears from my face. "How were you supposed to realize? You're a child."

"Mama. I'm not. Not anymore. You can talk to me about these things." I wipe my face and catch my breath. "Is that why you didn't leave?"

"I suppose so, yes. First, I was worried about leaving you completely alone. Then I was too sick to leave. But also, to be perfectly honest, I thought that any other life would have broken you and Mila for good. I thought that if I walked away from this life, I'd destroy you forever. That little girl looks at her father and sees him as a god. She sees him as good. You're old enough to know better, but even you are broken now." She looks at me. "I thought about leaving—believe me. Especially when I was sick."

"That's why you went back to school?"

"And that's why I kicked him out this year."

"I thought he left."

"No," she says with a quiet laugh. "Not at all."

"Then why is he back?"

"You haven't been well," she says. "I thought you needed your father."

"Oh, Mama, what am I supposed to do now?" I'm crying again. "How can you expect me to trust anyone? Or Mila? What are we supposed to do?"

"Look." She grabs a box of Kleenex from my nightstand, hands me a few tissues, and then wipes her eyes. "There are good people in the world. Whoever she grows up to love—whoever you grow up to love—let that person be good to you. You will have to. You will have to trust that person. You will just have to make that choice."

"Mama"—I take a deep breath—"are you going to leave him?"

She drops her head. "Oh, Viviana. I don't know. I think I will stay with him until I am finished with my degree, until you are done with college and Mila is old enough to understand a divorce. I think we will stay together for the good of the family."

"Which family?" I'm instantly sorry for saying it.

"Viviana. Do not be sarcastic. Not about this."

I sit up. "I'm completely serious. Please don't stay together for the 'good of the family.' That's not a good reason. Not at all."

She doesn't respond to this. She bites her lip and then looks at me.

"Please, Mama. Don't tell me you stayed for Mila and me. It's not fair of you to put it on us. We didn't ask for you to stay."

"Why do you think I'm in school? Why do you think I'm starting over in the middle of my life? It's so you and Mila can see that starting over is possible. That life doesn't end just because your heart is broken."

"Okay, so that means you're going to leave him, then, right?"

She doesn't answer my question. Instead, she looks me straight in the eye and says, "You understand, don't you? That's why I pushed you so hard all this time. I came here with nothing. I wanted everything. And then, when you were born, I wanted everything for *you*."

I think about this. Her life. Her choices. The pressures she's put on me to be better than her. "You had no right to shame me for what I did with Dean." I don't know where this comes from, but I know it's something I have to say. That I should have said months ago.

"Lower your voice, please."

"I'm sorry, but it's not fair. You can't do what you've done and then go and judge me."

"Viviana, please understand. That's why it hurt so bad, to see you make that mistake. I wanted better for you. I've always known you could do better than I have."

"I don't know what to say to that."

"Say that you understand. That you understand where I'm coming from."

I don't know that I can.

There's a gentle knock at the door.

"Mama? Vivi? Can I come in?"

My mom looks at me.

I nod. "Let her in."

She gets up and opens the door. "Yes, honey. You can. Come join us. We're done talking for now."

Mila climbs into my bed in between my mom and me. She doesn't ask what we were talking about. She just cuddles in under the blankets and lets us rub her head. She falls asleep first, and then my mom follows soon after. I lie awake for a while, staring at these two people: my mother, my sister. My father may be gone from my world, but I still have them. They still love me.

I think about everything my mom told me. I want to be angry with her. But I also want to understand her.

I don't know that I'll ever understand.

I do know that I love her, even if I don't agree with what she's done.

I lean my head against the window. The sky turns dark, and the city lights up.

I'm home.

When I wake up the next morning, my bed is empty. I make my way to the front room, but no one's there. I remember it's a weekday. My mom's at work and Mila's at camp.

There's a drawing on the table from Mila. It's the three

of us—my mom, Mila, and me—as stick figures. We're holding hands on a line of grass. There are two rainbows over our heads and heart-shaped raindrops falling from the white puffy clouds in the sky.

My dad's not anywhere in the drawing.

Mila's right. She's much smarter than any of us give her credit for.

I put the picture on the fridge.

Even though Evan must think I'm a hot mess, especially now that he has the whole story about my idiotic transgressions, he was right, I think.

I'm going to be okay.

And Mila's going to be okay, too.

"Did you talk to him?"

"No. We just messaged."

"What did he say?"

We're sitting on Sammie's balcony. We haven't talked about our fight. I tried to start with that, but she just pulled me out here so we wouldn't wake her mom.

Sammie reaches into her pocket and pulls out the phone. "Here."

Virgo: *Is this really Viviana?*

Sammie: *Please delete it.*

Virgo: *Evan didn't believe me.*

Sammie: *Pleeeeeeeease delete it.*

Virgo: *I will. I promise.*

I hand it back to her. She slides it into her pocket. "I deleted the photo, too."

"Again."

"Yes."

"This is going to follow me the rest of my life, isn't it?"

"I don't know, Vivi. . . ."

"I'm sorry I make you crazy with my drama—"

Sammie takes my hand and squeezes it. "Stop. Just stop. We both said mean things."

"Yes," I say. "We did."

"We're both impulsive, okay? It's what makes us *us*."

I nod. "I talked to my mom."

"You did?"

"Impulsively, yes." I tell Sammie about the conversation. "I don't know what's going to happen with them, but I'm going to ask her to demand that my dad pay for me to go to therapy."

"Oh?"

"I can't keep dumping on you."

"You can always dump on me, but I think it would help to have someone else—someone who knows what the hell they're doing—"

"To help me figure out what the hell I'm doing," I say.

"Exactly."

"I agree completely."

I get a text from my mom: *I thought I should call you: Your father's coming home early. He'll be here tonight. I understand that you might want to stay at Sammie's, but I do think you should talk. I won't be home until later, but I can try to schedule a sleepover for Mila at her friend's house. Let me know.*

I show Sammie the message. "What do you think? Should I start figuring it out tonight?"

"It's up to you."

Yes, I text back. *Do that. I want to see him.*

My father's obviously nervous. He's doing that thing where he shifts his glasses on his face and then coughs and shifts them again.

"What did you want to talk to me about?"

I'm looking at my father, and I don't see the god that Mila sees or the once-handsome grad student my mom fell in love with. I see a pockmarked, wrinkled, sad old man. The lies of his life, the stress of his life, they weigh down on him. He's hunched and tired.

"How was Acapulco?"

My father shudders at this. "What are you talking about? I was in Singapore."

"No," I say. "You were with Paige. And Ella. And your other kids."

My father pushes his chair back and stands up. "Who told you?" He pounds his fist on the table. "Did your mother tell you?"

"No, Dad. You might want to put a pass code on your phone."

He sits back down in his chair. "Son of a—"

"Do you love her?"

"Who?"

"Oh my God. Mom, of course."

He slumps over the table. He gets quiet and still.

"Did you *ever* love her?"

"One day you'll understand."

"Dad, what the hell kind of answer is that? One day I'll understand *what*, exactly?"

He lifts his head and looks at me. "Responsibility, complications. It's life as you know it, and you're comfortable enough to be petrified of any other version. You're close enough to withstand the other's habits—even if it involves other entanglements—to be okay with your own version of love. You're committed to this and there are other people—other hearts—involved. And what? Are you going to destroy their lives because of your principles? There are no principles. There's only survival."

"What does that even mean?" I want to cry or maybe laugh or maybe scream or maybe hit him. "Screw that, Dad! Talk to me. Answer my question: Did you ever love her? Or was your love just another lie?"

He doesn't answer.

"Oh my God. Do you even feel bad about everything you've done to us? To them?"

He pushes his glasses up his nose and leans toward me. "There's this concept—did you study it in your summer program thing?—called the 'hindsight bias.' We have it all the time in the engineering world. You can have all this data about the resisting forces that might weigh on your building—whether it's gravity, wind, temperature, erosion— you still don't know before you implement it what the real outcome will be. It's easy to go back to a failed design and say 'I would have done this differently' or 'I would have done that differently.' It's easy to piece the failure together later. We can predict a lot, more than ever, but the reality is that every structure in this world will fall down eventually. We still can't predict the exact moment of collapse."

"Are you saying we were a design experiment?"

"I'm saying that human impulses are larger than any physical reality. It's impossible to make predictions about a human life. You just never know what the right answer is. You never know exactly what the outcome will be." He looks at me. "I certainly couldn't have predicted this."

"Dad, are you ever able to give a straightforward answer?"

"I am not a liar, if that's what you want to know. I have been honest about my love for all of you."

"You know what? I can see that. I think you perceive the world as you want to. Someone else, who doesn't know you as well, might say you're lying to us, to the world. But the very sad truth is, you're lying to yourself." I push back my chair and stand up. "And *you're* the one who's going to collapse."

"What do you want me to say?" He stands up and hovers over me with his height, with his anger. "I'm your father, and you can't change that."

"No," I say. "You're right. I can't."

"What do you want from me?"

"To go live your life with Paige and your other, perfect family. I want you to leave Mom alone. To leave us alone."

"You know I can't do that," he says. "Your mother wants me here."

"You're only going to hurt Mila worse if you stay."

He shifts uncomfortably. "Are you going to tell her?"

I hear myself say, "I'm not sure yet. I mean, she'll find out eventually."

He looks down at the table. "You disappoint me, Viviana."

"Dad, I'm always disappointing you. All you ever wanted was for me to be like you, to be smart like you, to be *exactly* like you."

"I never said I wanted you to be like me." He looks up at me, adjusts his glasses again. "I said I wanted you to learn from your past mistakes, to learn from my past mistakes."

"Dad, even you don't know how to do that."

I grab my bag and storm out of the apartment. This time, he doesn't follow, thank goodness. I'm able to leave him there, alone with his twisted concepts and ridiculous theories about love and human impulses and right and wrong answers.

I run to the stairwell and let the door slam behind me.

But I don't know where I want to go. Not Sammie's. Not the pool. Not the endless, wandering streets.

I do know that I need to be alone.

I head up the stairs. There are twenty-one floors between the roof and me. I could take the elevator, but I feel like I need this walk upward. I assume that, despite my father's crazy talk, the engineers of this building calculated that it won't fall down today. I assume it's strong enough to hold me, even with the weight of my burdens and regrets.

I feel this deep need to push against gravity, against my father's sick and twisted ideas about how the world works, about how life works.

So I walk up and up and up.

———

I return to my apartment a few hours later and find my father's gone. I find my mom on the balcony, alone with a glass of wine. I open the sliding door. "Can I join you?"

She nods.

"Did you talk to him?"

"Yes."

"And?"

"It is over. I will not allow him to lie to us anymore."

I sit down next to her. "Really?"

"Yes," she says, taking a sip from her glass. "Really. I got the cancer removed from my neck. Now I will remove your father from my life. He is another kind of cancer."

I sit back in my chair. "What about Mila?"

"She will see him when he is in town. But he will not stay here."

"Oh."

"You can see him, too, if you want."

"I don't want to."

"Okay." She nods. "But he will pay for your college. He's promised me that."

I take a deep breath, try to hold back the tears. "What college? Dad was right. No one's going to accept me, not after what I did."

She puts down her glass. "You will get in somewhere. Plus, there are many options, many routes toward many different futures."

"I don't think so, Mama." I think about Virgo's texts to Sammie. "That picture has me doomed."

"Viviana, no." She reaches her arm around my shoulders. "You are so very young. Your life has only just begun. Don't let your mistakes define you."

I want to believe her. I want to so much.

The tears start to come. The tears and the nausea and the dizziness.

The city below us sways and swirls.

"I don't know, Mama—"

"Come here, honey." She pulls me toward her. I rest my head against her chest. The tears come fast, but I don't try to hold them back. "It's okay. You can cry. Let it out."

So I do.

I cry until I'm nearly out of breath. My mother rubs my back. She doesn't tell me to calm down or stop crying or anything. She just lets me be.

Finally, when I feel like I've run dry, I lift my head. "Are you getting a divorce, then?"

My mom looks at me. "Viviana, there is no divorce."

"What? Why not?"

"Oh, honey. Don't you get it? We were never married."

"Oh, Mama. I didn't realize."

She goes on to explain that it will be a clean break, one that won't require lawyers or courts or papers signed and certified. He will just be gone. He will just disappear. "I had hoped that you would never find out. I'm so sorry, Viviana. There are so many things I would have done differently if I could have."

I shake my head. "Don't let your mistakes define you."

She strokes my hair. "You make me very proud, Viviana. Thank you for pushing me. Thank you for believing in me."

She reaches out for a hug, and I hold her in close. I feel like this is the first time we've ever really talked to each other. I feel like I never want to let go.

"I want to go to therapy," I whisper. "I need to talk about all of this with someone."

"Yes," she says, sitting back. "He will pay for that, too, at least until I am finished with school. And then I will take care of it all myself."

"I have all the money from my job."

"No. That's your money. If he doesn't come up with the money, I'll find a way to pay for it as long as you need it."

"Thank you, Mama."

"No, Viviana." My mom reaches her hands out to mine. "Thank you."

College Essay Tip

Offer a specific, authentic experience from your life. Provide details from your life so that the colleges can get to know you as an individual.

Viviana Rabinovich-Lowe
Common Application
FINAL DRAFT

Prompt: Mainly, colleges want to see that, while you've made mistakes in your life, you have grown from these mistakes and will use the lessons to function as a mature college student. Write about a mistake you've made and the lessons you've learned as a result.

I'm on the cusp. And it's so scary. I'm about to leave high school, enter the world of college and everything that comes after. I will be expected to "function as a mature *college student." The question is: Considering the mistakes that I've made, can I do it?*

My whole life could open up, and it could go in a million different amazing or horrible directions, but I don't know. I don't know which way to turn. My mother says I'm the one to determine my tomorrows, but that seems like too much. Too much power. Too much control. This life is too wild for me to have any say. This life is too strange, too wonderful and horrible. It's too much all at once, sometimes.

I did make a mistake—a grave one—during my junior year of high school, one that has followed me for months, and one that might very well follow me the rest of my life. I trusted someone with some personal information, and he proceeded to share this information with the world. Soon after, I discovered some truths about my family, deep, dark secrets that made me question who I am, where I come from, what I am made of. But that is all I want to say about both debacles.

That being said, I've learned so very much because of it. For a while, I thought I'd never trust anyone again. But I will. I already do. There's definitely one person in this world I know I can count on. She's there in the mirror. And if I listen to my heart, if I trust in that voice that sits deep in my soul, that untouched being of truth—I know it's there—I will discover the answers eventually. Maybe not immediately. Maybe not tomorrow. But if I don't open myself to possibility, I'll never know what it means to have lived. I'll never know what it means to have loved.

I refuse to live like those who have betrayed me. I refuse to succumb to bitterness and fear. I refuse to waste any more of my precious time waiting for some semblance of a life. I

will live this life the only way I know how. With love at its
core. With love in my heart.

The rest will be made real in time.

The rains finally let up and the next few days are sunny and hot and humid; it's August in full force. Sammie's mom announces that she's secured a new job and a new apartment, and they start to pack. I don't stay over there anymore since I'm happy to be home, finally, but I do spend evenings up at their place, partly so I can help, partly so I can get in as much time with Sammie as possible. School doesn't start until after Labor Day, in September, but the date weighs heavily on me. I don't want her to move.

Mila's grumpy because our dad's gone again. My mom has a long talk with her. She doesn't tell her why Dad's left, but she promises that he'll be back, and while it's not the complete truth, it's enough for Mila right now. Eventually, we'll have to tell her everything. Eventually, she'll have to know.

I don't see Evan all weekend. He's not at work—apparently, he called in sick, and Sammie hasn't heard anything else from Virgo about the picture.

"I can't delete my past," I say to Sammie one night as we're packing up her stuff. "He either accepts me for who I am—nudie pic and all—or he doesn't, and then I don't need him in my life."

"It's glad to see you finally owning it," Sammie says, laughing. "Nudie pic and all. That's awesome."

"What else am I going to do?" I say. "I can't lie about it. This is who I am. Who I was. It'll always be a part of me."

I say it like I mean it, but the reality is, I'm nervous about seeing Evan. Virgo hasn't said anything to me, and he's treating me like normal, which is reassuring, but I don't have a complicated relationship with Virgo. He's my boss and my friend. That's it. I haven't kissed him three times and then promptly showed him my crazy.

Evan's back at work on Tuesday, but I hardly see him. The sun and high temperatures have seemingly brought the entire Bennett Village out to the pool, as though every single family with all of their kids and extended families is here, like they've all skipped work and camp to come swim. Virgo orders two guards on deck at a time, which means Evan's doing double shifts.

At the end of the day, he comes into the office, sees me, says an awkward hello, and then grabs his guitar and leaves.

"Well," I say to Sammie later. "He's one for the history books. So much for friendship. I guess I am on my own this year."

She crawls onto her bed. "I'm sorry I'm leaving."

"Would you stop apologizing?" I sit down next to her. "It's not your fault."

"What are you going to do without me?" Sammie says it with a laugh, but I know the question is real.

"I'm less worried about myself and more worried about the Drama Department. Who's going to be their lead this year? Have you told them you're not going back?"

"Don't remind me. It's the only reason I've decided to enroll at the school in Morton Grove. Well, that and the fact that my mom and I negotiated that I could have my Instagram account back after she saw that all my photos *really were* about fashion."

"No GED?"

"Nah. My mom convinced me to give it a few months, and if I don't like it, I can try for my certificate."

"Good."

"Why good?"

"I'd miss seeing you onstage."

"What about you?" Sammie says. "What's your plan for survival this year?"

I shrug. "Join the Olympiads. Take Physics Two. Learn coding so I can avoid any future online scandals. Embrace the reality that I like my science classes, even though it's something that would please my dad."

"Ha. As long as you don't stress too much about it."

"I'm going to try not to."

"Good. What about make new friends?"

"Yes. I'll probably try that, too."

Sammie leans her head on my shoulder. "Good."

I lean over her and reach for my bag. "I've got something for you."

"It's my birthday present!" Sammie starts to wiggle and clap her hands before I can even get to it. "Gimme, gimme!"

"Oh my God. How did you know?" I say, laughing.

"Leos are psychic. You know that."

"Well, I didn't before, but now I do." I pull it out of my bag and hand it to her. "It's not quite a scavenger hunt. I hope it'll do."

There are two boxes. Sammie surprises me by unwrapping them slowly, with care, despite her initial excitement. Inside the first one is a beaded gold headband and a book called *The Art of the Braid*, which makes Sammie smile. "I love them both," she says.

"Our braiding sessions will never end."

Inside the second box is the real present. "Oh, Viviana," she whispers. "Where did you get these?"

It's a mosaic of our friendship, sixteen photos from when we were kids all the way through this last year, hung on four lines with clothespins, in one large frame, all artistic, the way Sammie likes. My mom let me copy the framed Instagram photos she had on her dresser, the ones of Sammie and me, as we were before this last year happened. "These are the photos that matter," I say. "It's a record of us. For your new room."

She clutches it tight to her chest and starts to cry. "This is perfect. The absolute best present I've ever gotten from anyone, ever."

"I can't believe you're really leaving."

Sammie shakes her head, like she doesn't want to talk about it. She wraps the frame I made in some bubble wrap and slides it into an open cardboard box. "The O'Briens were eating fondue last night," she whispers.

"No way," I say. I get it. She's changing the subject because it's too hard to talk about the future, about what's coming next. There are so many unknowns, and so many possibilities. Sometimes there are things you can say, and talking makes it better. But sometimes, there are no words.

"Yup," she continues. "They were all sitting around the

dining room table, dipping strawberries in a fountain of chocolate."

"How civilized of them."

"Right?" she says, laughing now through her tears. "Oh, and Mrs. Woodley's moving out!"

"What?"

"He was there! The muscular gym rat guy, her new lover."

"You're lying to me."

"I'm not!" She lifts her fingers. "Scout's honor. I saw them last night. He was helping her move."

"Are you sure he's not her son or nephew or something?"

"I'm one hundred percent sure. They were making out."

"I don't know if I believe you."

"I wouldn't lie to you. Really. Not after everything you've been through."

I grab her and hug her tight. "I'm really happy for Mrs. Woodley."

She squeezes me back. "So am I."

When I arrive at work the next day, it's raining again. It's still hot and humid, and it's nothing like the storms of a few weeks ago, so while the pool isn't empty, it's not packed, either. Sammie's in Morton Grove, registering for her new school, and I'm alone today, which doesn't suck as bad as it used to.

I find Evan sitting at the front desk. He's on break and deep in conversation with Professor Cox, who's perched on the counter, spouting off philosophies about the world. "You want to know life's incredible hoax?"

"Yes, Professor Cox," Evan says with a laugh. "I most certainly do."

"All of this—" Professor Cox sweeps his hands through the air. "Is an illusion. Don't take it too seriously. If you do, you'll just set yourself up for heartbreak. A lifetime of heartbreak."

I take a seat next to Evan at my post. He doesn't say anything, but he does nod at me and then he gives me a smile that seems genuine. Professor Cox is going on and on about "silence and light and connections made in the shadows of our beings." Most of it doesn't make sense. Some of it does.

Evan listens and nods and asks for definitions and clarifications while I check in visitors and sell bags of Cheetos to little kids.

"I told my parents about my major."

I nearly slam the money drawer on my own hand. "What?"

"It's why I wasn't here last weekend. I told them."

"Good for you, my lad," Professor Cox says.

I shut the drawer. "How'd they take it?"

Evan looks at me and laughs. "They freaked out. Well, my dad did. He lost his temper and threatened to stop paying for my college."

"It's to be expected," Professor Cox says. "You cannot live your life for them."

"My dad started slurring his speech and we had to take him to the ER. Turns out he didn't have another stroke, but he came close."

"Oh my God," I say.

"I stood up to him, though. By the end of the weekend,

he came to terms with it. Well, mostly. My mom told him it wasn't worth dying over, that it was just music. She also made me promise that I'd think about minoring in business so I don't get screwed over by record companies."

Professor Cox nods. "Mick Jagger studied at the London School of Economics."

"That's so random. How do you know this stuff?" Evan asks.

Professor Cox points to his head. "I have an exceptional brain with great capacities for retaining information, both useful and useless. It is a blessing and a curse."

"I wish I had that kind of brain."

"But you do." Professor Cox smiles. "For music."

"I'm glad for you," I say.

"Thanks." Evan looks at me. "I did it because of you."

"What do you mean—"

"Evan!" Virgo yells from the deck before Evan can answer. "Can you come here! I think there's a turd in the water."

Evan smiles at me and then runs to the water.

Professor Cox looks at me. "It's nice to see two people in love."

"Oh, no." I shake my head. "We're not in love. Not at all." I shuffle some papers. "Anyway, I thought you didn't believe in love."

"Romantic love, no. But there are many different kinds of love in this world. You can be intimate with someone and call it a friendship. You can be passionate with someone and call it a romantic relationship, which is the one I don't believe in, since it's the one that both occurs and fails the most. But if you combine intimacy and passion with the precious third material that involves honesty and trust—you can achieve a kind of love that is very rare in this world. I don't know much about you and Mr. Whitlock, but I see that you are honest with each other. He trusts you."

"He does?"

"You don't see it?"

I look out toward the pool at Evan.

"Like I said, I have an exceptional brain, and I can tell you that with one hundred percent certainty, that boy loves you. Perhaps you might open your eyes so you can see it, too."

The pool is shut down again early, this time for fear of contamination from "the fecal incident," as Virgo is now calling it. The water is evacuated, and except for the few committed sunbathers, everyone leaves, including Professor Cox.

I stay at the front desk to let newcomers know that the pool is closed but that they are welcome to relax on deck. I'm met with groans and dirty looks, as though I'm the one who had diarrhea in the water.

"Thanks for staying," Virgo says as he puts the lock on the gate for final closing.

"It's no problem."

"Am I locking you in, or locking you out?"

I look over at Evan. He's stacking chairs against the wall. "I need to talk to Evan for a minute."

"Good," Virgo says. "Finally."

I laugh. "What does that mean?"

"Nothing," Virgo says. "It's just—you've made an impression on him."

I'm not sure if he means the photo or me, but I don't ask him.

Instead, I walk over to Evan.

"Hey. We need to talk."

Evan throws a chair on the stack and looks at me. "Okay. Now?"

"Yes, now," I say. "I know you saw the picture."

"Okay. I did. But—"

"And I don't know what you think of me, but frankly, I don't care. I mean—I don't care if you're judging me or whatever."

"I'm not—"

"This is who I am. I am honest, unlike my father. And when I am in love—which I *was* with Dean—I am honest with my love, as well. It was an absolutely honest photo that was meant to be shared only with him. Maybe I'm too trusting, but I can't change that about myself, as much as I'd like to."

"I'm not judging you. I don't care about that photo. I don't care about any of that."

"You don't?"

"No, Viviana. I like you. That's it, okay? I like you. And I'd like us to get to know each other better. Maybe hang out more. Maybe kiss more in normal places and without it ending in you yelling at me."

"Oh," I say. I take a seat on a lounge chair. "I like you, too. I guess that's why I'm telling you all this."

He sits down next to me. "Would you like to hang out

sometime, maybe Extreme Ping-Pong or Extreme Billiards or something like that?"

"Does it have to be extreme?"

Evan laughs. "Not at all."

"Then yes." I nod. "I'm in a weird, fragile place right now. But I'd like that."

"Great."

"Are you free right now?"

I hear a voice above. I look up at Bennett Tower. Professor Cox is on his balcony. He's singing "The Ants Go Marching"; his uneven voice echoes over the city. Virgo steps out of the office and joins in; his voice overtakes Professor Cox's. It's deep and beautiful, even while he sings a silly child's song.

I scan the tower. My mother is upstairs on the sixteenth floor, probably studying for her law exam and cooking for Mila and me. I expect Sammie's also home by now, packing up her room. I imagine the O'Briens with their fondue and Mrs. Woodley with her younger man.

"I am," I say. "I am free."

I'm free to live my life and love my life any way I want, as long as it's with kindness and honesty and an open, trusting heart.

I see that now.

That it's my life to live.

And mine alone.

ACKNOWLEDGMENTS

For me, each book begins with a question. Along the way, that question breeds other questions, and I am seriously one lucky girl to have so many people I can go to for answers.

Courtney Miller-Callihan at Handspun Literary! (Woot!) Thank you for your friendship and your guidance. We are one lucky (not-so-secret) club to have you as our leader.

So much gratitude to Rose Hilliard, for believing in me and for asking me to follow this story. It's been the greatest pleasure to be cheered on and guided by you over these past two years. Thank you for everything.

Many thanks to everyone at St. Martin's Press, including Brittani Hilles, Angelique Giammarino, Brant Janeway, Jen Enderlin, Anne Marie Tallberg, David Curtis, Talia Sherer, Anne Spieth, Karen Masnica, and Jennie Conway.

Dana Kaye, thank you for guiding me through my debut year.

To my beta and sensitivity readers: Matthew Frey, my first reader, always (plus you get to be listed twice!), Nicole Brinkley, Karlyn Westover, Jessica Love, Ron Romasanta, and Anna Davis. Thank you, Julie Caplan Nuzzalo, Psy.D., for your expertise, insights, and suggestions.

My soul sisters: Kate Eberle, Aimee Kandelman, and Kara Noe, for our four million daily texts. So many questions, so many (usually right) answers. I'll always ask you first.

All of my amazing writing friends (you know who you are). These last two years. Oh, boy. Thank you for letting me cry and telling me to breathe and making me laugh and hugging me hard. Seriously, thank you. Without you, I'd be lost. Special thanks to Jessica Love, Charlotte Huang, Amy Spalding, and Laurie Elizabeth Flynn for reading this book early and lending your support. (P.S. Amy: thanks for the weekly check-ins!) Special thanks to L. M. Klein and the Binders for coming up with the best possible title.

Christy Marsden, I'll never stop thanking you.

To everyone at Pasadena City College. There are too many people to list here, which means that I am ridiculously blessed. And I must thank my students. You're the ones who keep me learning, writing, and laughing, so thank you. Deborah Bird, Salomon Davida, and Sandy Lee for our work with DesignTech! You've taught me so much. And to Amy Ulmer, Vanitha Swaminathan, Sam Swaminathan, Kathleen Green, and Terri Keeler, for your constant enthusiasm and support.

To all of the readers, librarians, teachers, booksellers, bloggers, and fans who have reached out and supported my writing. Again, I am truly, ridiculously blessed.

To my family, for surrounding me with love: Ray Elias, Shirley Mann, Chuck Bush, Karnit Galmidi, and Michael Braun. Mom and Dad, wherever you are, I know you know.

And always, the most gratitude to the two loves of my life, Madeline and Matthew. Thank you for your trust and support and for living the questions with me.